RITE OF GRACE

A WILLOW GRACE MYSTERY
BOOK 7

C.C. WEST

WITHOUT WARRANT

Willow Grace FBI Thrillers

CONTENT WARNING

This book covers a myriad of potentially distressing subjects
including but not limited to:

Organ trafficking — on page.
Blood/gore — on page.
Occult practices — on page.
Cult survivors — referenced.
Overdosing — referenced.

Readers' discretion is advised.

1

The Keeper of Knowledge

Earth bless the matriarch.

The Keeper of Knowledge shuffled around the room, rubbing his cold fingertips across his dry palms in agitation. His eyes kept landing on the ancient book lying open on the table, everything in him desperate to deny the implications.

He walked towards the table and looked down at the open pages, rereading the entry. He flipped to the pages before and after, just to check, just to be absolutely sure. Yet there could only be one reason for her to have consulted *that* book. That damning entry. He had been up all night, thinking it over. There was no hiding this evidence.

The Keeper started pacing again. No surely, *surely* he was wrong. He didn't want to think this was true, that she could be planning something so heinous. Not after the matriarch had joined the Earth again, and so recently. Had they all not been pained enough? Had the matriarch's death not—

He stopped short, halted mid-stride in the middle of the room, facing the fireplace with his back to the only door. The pages of the books lining the walls to his left and right had stopped whispering to him. The concoctions he had been brewing on the desk opposite the fireplace had stopped bubbling. Even the dying fire had stopped crackling. Silence consumed him, like the deep breath before a battle cry.

Someone was here.

He rolled his shoulders as he waited, the sound of soft footsteps across the grass outside thunderous amidst the stark silence. The door creaked open and he inhaled a deep breath through his nose. He could smell her perfume, luscious and hazy.

"Kay," she said, her smooth voice like dripping butter.

"My lady," the Keeper replied, still facing the fire. "What brings you back to my abode this night?"

"I-I wanted to explain," she said. "My behavior when you found me here earlier."

The Keeper let out a wry chuckle. "What is there to explain? You were seeking knowledge." He shrugged, glancing just past his shoulder to see her in his periphery. "'Tis what people come to me and my library for, is it not?"

The floor squeaked as if she had shifted her weight. "Of course, but—"

"What else could there be to explain, my lady?" He walked to the table and picked up the open book from the middle. The book flopped open even wider as he raised it up. "Is it that you want to explain why you sought information from one of our most ancient texts? Texts only the matriarch—Earth bless her—and myself are permitted to read?" The Keeper turned to face her. "You know it is forbidden, my lady."

He let the book drop, and it hit the floor with a hollow thud, still open to the incriminating entry.

She looked at the book on the ground before raising her eyes to meet his. Her countenance held no remorse, no fear. Voice deepening, she said, "You know as well as I that there will be a new matriarch."

"And you think it will be you?"

She spread her arms wide. "I am her chosen. It is my right."

"Yet you wish to take it by force through forbidden magic?" The Keeper's voice grew thunderous. "You thought I wouldn't notice? You think me a fool? Your secret wasn't long kept from me."

And then she leered at him, her mouth shrinking into a thin line as she revealed her teeth. "Then you, o grand and all-knowing one, know why I'm really here."

The Keeper laughed without humor. "You think the summit will protect you if you do this?"

"The summit will have no choice but to bow to me." She pulled out a long dagger from under her cloak. "But not before your blood drenches the earth."

And she kicked the book aside, before lunging forward, dagger glinting in the firelight. She aimed for his ribs, but the Keeper dodged her attack with ease. She stumbled across the room behind him, nearly colliding into the wall. She whirled around, growling.

"You'll have to do better than that, my lady." He pulled his own knife from his belt and held it in front of him.

She attacked again, charging with her dagger towards him, but again he stepped to the side. This time she caught herself before she tumbled on her feet. She swung her dagger upright, feinting, and arched the dagger towards his kidney but he blocked her, pushing her back hard enough that she fell to the floor. As she rolled away, he grabbed the book off the floor and bolted to the door.

"No!" She cried, manicured hands reaching after him.

He pulled the door open and ran out into the twilight. A car had pulled up to the building, its lights flooding the front porch, lighting his path forward into the forest. He almost missed the sound of one of the car doors opening.

The sound of the front door bouncing off its hinges clapped through the air. "Get him! Don't let him escape!"

She had brought someone with her.

He had made it to the woods, thinking he was safe, thinking he could hide amidst the trees when a shot rang out, and a red-hot pain consumed his left shoulder. He cried out and collapsed to the forest floor, the tome tumbling from his grasp. The earth spun under him and it was all he could do to keep himself from retching.

"There's no escaping, Kay." Her buttery voice filled the air, echoing off the trees. "You won't be able to stop me from taking my rightful place."

"You think this is what the matriarch would have wanted?" The Keeper shouted back, biting down the agony of rent flesh.

Another shot rang out, and a sharp rush of air blew against his ear as the bullet just missed him. A large figure pushed its way through the underbrush and the Keeper guessed that this was whomever she had brought with her.

An accomplice? Another traitor?

The roaring of blood in his ears drowned out the two sets of footsteps behind him. Nettles stung his hands as he tried pushing himself up, only to lose his balance and crash into the ground again, this time onto his throbbing shoulder. He stifled a groan as sweat dripped down his forehead. But her betrayal hurt more than anything else.

The summit. He had to tell the summit what she had done, what she was doing. He had to get to the estate.

Breath catching in his lungs, the Keeper pushed himself up again, screaming as a twig caught at the bullet hole. He scrambled forward and grabbed the book. The forest around him grew darker by the second, the only light coming from the flashlights of his assailants.

Holding his now sticky, wet shoulder with his right hand, the book under his left elbow, he looked behind him again to see the two figures gaining on him. He made sure of his footing on the sloping ground, sticks and brush poking through his clothes, leaving stinging welts as he dashed forward.

This couldn't be how it ended. He couldn't fail his matriarch. Couldn't let this be the fate of the coven.

The Keeper's heart stopped as his foot, instead of hitting the solid, leaf-covered ground, plunged forward into nothingness. He screamed as he tumbled over the edge of a sudden drop off. Head over feet, he fell forward, rolling down the hill so fast he lost all semblance of which way was up or down, rolling without ceasing, until it all came to abrupt explosion of stars and an excruciating pain in his head. He tasted blood, smelled the earth plugging his nose.

"Kay!" A voice cried behind him.

Earth bless the matriarch. Forgive me.

2

Willow

A few weeks ago...

THE DOOR HISSED OPEN. I WALKED INTO THE INTERROGATION room, now familiar to me from all the hours I'd spent inside it over the winter. Stale coffee-scented air from the hallway dissipated into the dead, sterile air of the stark chamber. The faint flickering florescent light fixture above Terrance Kincaid cast his face into a harsh shadow, putting in mind a hunter viewing his prey.

I'd often wondered if this was how his personal victims had seen him—hungry and calculating.

"What a pleasure it is to see you again, Dr. Grace." Kincaid grinned at me as the door hissed shut behind me.

He was seated in his usual spot, behind the table facing the one-way window. Feet outstretched under the table, manacled hands resting on the tabletop, he seemed more relaxed than usual. He must have been briefed on why we'd requested this emergency meeting with him. It would explain the excessive smugness.

I walked over to my usual seat and pulled it away from the table. Glancing at the door behind Kincaid, I caught a glimpse of a security guard standing by, waiting in the middle walkway between the door and the secure facility beyond. My hands were clammy, making my pen stick to my palm for a millisecond as I dropped it on top of my notebook.

Kincaid pulled his feet back as I took my seat. He sat upright and interlaced his fingers, smiling at me from across the table. Despite the calm demeanor I was trying so hard to present I could see in his eyes that he wasn't buying it. He watched me as I took several deep, slow inhales, before sitting back in my seat.

I met his gaze. Same widow's peak, though his hair shaved now, compared to its shoulder-length when we had first met. He was paler too, now that he was spending so much time locked in a private cell. But that smirk and those smug eyes, glittering as if relishing in secrets he'd already pried open, were the same as ever.

He smiled at me. "You seem tense, Dr. Grace."

Damn him. Damn them for convincing me to come.

"Your previous intel was helpful," I said, glancing at my watch. I picked up my pen again.

"Just helpful?"

"Incredibly helpful, actually."

Kincaid inclined his head. "I'm glad to hear it. Now, have you thought about your answer to my question?"

I had. Too much so.

"Yes," I told him. "But there's hardly anything to relate. At least nothing that would be of interest to you."

Grin widening, he leaned forward, the metal chair creaking underneath him. "Come, Dr. Grace. You know the rules. *Quid Pro Quo* as the famed, flesh-hungry psychiatrist would say."

Ever since we had brought Terrance Kincaid—otherwise known as the Recruiter, a world-renowned criminal specialized in rallying people and toppling governments with cult brainwashing tactics—to

Seattle, it had been a constant battle of quid pro quo between the two of us.

To everyone's surprise, including my own, he wouldn't talk to anyone else in the bureau *except* for me. Or rather, I was the only one he wouldn't *completely* bullshit.

The only way that he was willing to reveal strands of the web he controlled was by learning more and more about me and my past. Which was a harder bargain that I had been willing to strike, as his questions included diving into my upbringing, my escape from the cult in which I grew up, the fear of being found out and dragged back to the nightmares I had run from. But as much as I hated being forced to open up to this man, the FBI needed him. If anyone else interrogated him, he'd give false or incomplete information which proved to be detrimental to the point of having informants vanish or nearly losing cops in several close calls. So, I relived long forgotten sections of my past to help topple his regime. I tucked my left leg under my right thigh and nodded, glancing at my watch again. "Any memories I had of my father have either been erased or are so dim in my mind, I don't know if they're real."

Kincaid leaned back in his chair, making a *tsk* noise with his tongue. "That's not good enough Dr. Grace."

I cast my gaze around the room, searching for something to say. Unfortunately for me, the gray room lit by a single pane of florescent lighting and bare of anything except the table and two chairs provided no inspiration, fictional or otherwise.

"Tall," I said after a moment. "He was tall, I think. Blue eyes? Maybe hazel? And—" I paused, worrying at my lower lip with my upper teeth. "A smile. A kind smile."

Goosebumps erupted on my arms and the interrogation room plummeted a further few degrees. Forcing myself not to begin tapping the table with my pen, I lowered it on the tabletop beside my notebook before lowering my hand under the table to wipe the sweat off on my corduroy pant suit.

Kincaid kept his hands on the table in front of him. "That's a little better."

I adjusted my glare to what I hoped was a diplomatic expression. Clearing my throat, I looked back down at my notebook and pulled it onto my propped leg. "Can you tell us anything more that would aid in the Rendezvous case?"

"My question first," Kincaid said. "You're about to look at your watch again. Why?"

I took my eyes off my watch and directed my gaze to Kincaid.

McCannon always advised against showing all your cards to this man. To never tell the whole truth, to lie where possible, and to always remain two steps ahead.

But we were out of time for me to be clever.

"Everything you've said has proven to be true and helpful. But at this very moment there are lives on the line. Every second we spend here could be another life—"

"Or limb," Kincaid said, smiling.

"Lost," I finished, faltering.

Kincaid hummed then went silent and still, eyes on the tabletop. He sat that way for a long time.

Threats, promises, pleas all raced through my mind but pushing him would result in him leaving without another word.

So I waited, controlling my breathing and preventing myself from tapping my pen to keep from showing my increasing, desperate impatience.

After a small eternity, Kincaid shifted in his seat. He took a deep breath and looked me in the eye.

"What you're looking for isn't what you actually seek, you know. You're looking for the answers. Just as any moral person would, but the men, the organization you're after? Are merely tools in the hands of someone *far* more competent. It's like saying you're looking for the lamb when you don't even know where the flock is."

"Respectfully, Mr. Kincaid," I said, working to keep my voice from shaking, "we don't have time to dissect half clues. I need something real, and I need something now."

"Dissect." He said the word slowly. "Interesting word choice, given the context, wouldn't you agree?"

I inhaled a long breath through my nose, tamping down the urge to scream.

The corner of Kincaid's mouth lifted. "But you're right. Time is of the essence. You're looking for an old processing plant, down by the bay. Went by the name of Planter's Meats. The people you're searching for use it as a surgical suite. You'll find them there but only if you're quick. I'd bring a mop if I were you."

Ignoring the last comment, I wrote the information down as fast as I could and stood, nearly knocking over my chair. "Thank you, Mr. Kincaid."

"And Doctor?"

I stopped by the door, my hand gripping the handle I'd already turned, and glanced back at him.

"Consider why and for whom the hearts are missing."

3

Holt

This wasn't going to be pretty.

Sitting across from me in the split aisled van was Marcus McCannon, our department head. He looked at ease in his black tactical gear, with his shoulders relaxed and his legs spread apart in front of him. He was going over the operation notes again.

"The operating suite is on the third floor, connected to the parking garage, so we'll be able to block off all exits." McCannon looked around the van. "I want this to be quick. In and out."

The team, consisting of myself and a handful of other agents, all nodded.

"Do you think Baily's alright, sir?" One agent asked.

McCannon remained facing forward. "I hope to God he is."

A fresh wave of dread settled on me as I rolled my shoulders. Once we had found where the traffickers were picking up donors, we needed someone to go undercover. Baily had been the first to volunteer. It would be my fault if anything happened to him.

"Do you think Kincaid's intel will check out?" I asked, hitting my leg with the side of my thumb.

McCannon nodded once. "Everything Grace has gotten for us has so far. The man doesn't stand to gain anything by lying to us."

"Except amusement," I said, casting a loaded glance at McCannon. "Willow says she can tell he's bored of being locked up."

She would never say it, but all the time she was spending with Kincaid was taking a toll on her. She always came away from their interviews more tense than before going in.

"However," McCannon said, "as much as he likes playing games, he's never outright lied. In spite of the faulty information he's given us in the past, he's also insisted that he wants to help the FBI in tackling this ring."

Leaning forward and resting my elbows on my knees, I said, "I still don't believe his reformed-cult-overlord bit."

"It'd be foolish to," McCannon agreed.

The van jostled and everyone bobbed up and down. I leaned back, holding onto my bullet proof vest, thinking of Willow's last words to me back at the bureau before the team had gotten into the van. She had grabbed my hand and, even now, the memory of her touch succeeded in relaxing my shoulders.

"You're gonna get Baily out," she had said. "Along with everyone else."

Ten minutes later we were parked in the parking garage, the ground team having already secured the perimeter and disabled the cameras.

All the agents filed out of the van, one after the other with Glocks or rifles in hand. I hopped out of the van and followed McCannon to the door leading to the stairwell.

"We have about two minutes before anyone notices the cameras are off," he said. "Let's go."

Guns in the ready position, we entered the building via the stairwell. Pot and urine filled the air. My colleagues scrunched their noses before sobering and pressing forward. Faded graffiti covered the walls. Trash and leaves crowded every corner.

Two of the team members walked down the stairs, evading the gum tacked all over the ground, as the rest of us crossed the short walkway to the third-floor entrance. A new security alarm was attached to the wall above the doorway. We waited until the light in the center turned from orange to green. The lock clicked, and the door opened half an inch.

I led the team into a darkened hallway. The rank air of the stairwell dissolved into cleaning chemicals. Bleach, ammonia, and pine. Cool central air thrummed through the vents. Light poured through two round windows, each in the high center of a pair of double metal doors at the end of the hall. I started towards them.

"See anything yet?" Litz, an agent downstairs, whispered into our earpieces, voice tinny in our earpieces.

"Nothing yet," McCannon replied.

"We've just come into a revamped storage room. Cooler boxes everywhere."

His voice was creaky from whispering. Then a soft thump followed by a curse came over the earpiece.

"What is it?" McCannon asked.

"It's a cooler full of kidneys, sir."

An image of Willow opening a freezer filled with limbs, followed by my niece wrapped in a blanket came to my mind. I blinked to dispel the memories and the twist in my stomach.

Another thump. "And a cooler of... what the hell is that? Livers?" Litz paused. "Shit."

"What, what is it?"

"They're still warm, sir."

"Keep looking," McCannon said. "They've got to be there."

We made our way to the double doors down the hall. I peered through the left window to see a large room, like that of an old hospital ward, filled with metal tables and curtained off areas. No sign of life.

"Clear," I said.

I pushed open the door and walked inside. Cold, sterile air hit me, making my eyes water. Disinfectant overpowered the air. A single, hanging light tinged the room yellow. A table rested beneath the light. A white cloth covered the surface. Something bulged from beneath the crimson-stained fabric.

The most prominent stain, glistening under the bulb's light, rested atop the center of a human torso. My mouth went dry as I walked up to the table. McCannon raised his hand at me as he directed another agent further into the room.

My teammate Centry walked past me to one of the six curtained off stalls. She pushed back the dingy privacy cloth to reveal an empty body bag. She pulled back the curtain of the next stall, then the next.

"They're all empty," she said, holding her earpiece.

Litz muffled a curse. "Where are the bodies then?"

"There's just the one." I looked down at the stained cloth beside me and turned the sheet down.

McCannon sidled up to me and swore.

Anger and horror rose up my esophagus in the form of bile. I couldn't tear my eyes away.

It was Baily. But not *all* of Baily. Both of his eyes were gone, gouged out of his head. My former sister-in-law flashed through my mind and I blinked hard to rid myself of the thought. Baily was—

Pulling the cloth down further revealed a cavity on the left side of his chest, right where his heart should have been. Blood had pooled inside the hole, coagulated around the edges.

"What is it?" Litz's voice came over the earpiece, his tone tense. "Have you found something?"

"We found Baily," Centry replied, voice flat. "What's left of him, anyways."

Recovering Baily with the cloth, I hissed, "Where the hell are the rest of the bodies?"

"We have to—"

Voices and footsteps sounded from behind the door across the room.

The door swung open. Two men in scrubs and face masks walked in, one laughing. They skidded to a stop at the sight of us. They screamed something in a foreign language and pulled guns from the holsters at their hips.

Then all hell broke loose.

4

A week later...

Willow

"You're tired, Dr. Grace," Kincaid said.

Nodding, I walked over to my usual place at the interrogation table and placed my notebook down, glancing at my watch. A quarter to three.

"Yes, it's been a long few days." I pulled the chair back and sat down. "McCannon wanted to express our gratitude for your intel."

Kincaid tilted his head. "I hope my intel proved useful in providing the whereabouts of... Agent Baily, wasn't it? I saw the news."

My stomach twisted, recalling the news coverage. "Then you saw that it did."

"And the Ring?"

"Dismantled."

"Any survivors?"

I lowered my gaze.

Kincaid made a tsk noise with his tongue. "Unfortunate. What about the traffickers?"

"That was the other reason McCannon sent me to talk to you today." I sat forward, opening my notebook. "Are you aware of any hideouts or places the traffickers would flee to?"

Kincaid shrugged and leaned back in his chair. "I couldn't tell you."

I studied him. His face was devoid of any hints that would allow me a glimpse into his thoughts. "Couldn't or won't?"

He met my gaze and another small smirk formed on his lips. "Lack of sleep seems to put you on edge, Dr. Grace."

No, your stupid mind tricks are putting me on edge.

But I decided not to say anything. Neither did he for a time. Then he changed the subject.

Running a finger along the edge of the table, he said, "What do you do with your free time, Dr. Grace?"

I leaned back in my chair too, mirroring his body language. "Is this part of our Quid Pro Quo?"

He laughed, a startling sound that was almost infectious. "You know what? Yes. Humor me. After you're done with work today, what do you plan on doing?"

Innocent enough question, but it had to be bait of some kind.

I decided to bite. "I'm meeting an old friend to have coffee."

"So late in the afternoon?"

I shrugged. "It was convenient for both of us."

Kincaid looked me over again from my face all the way to my feet, his gaze appraising in a way that a teacher would look over a student. "And where are you going to have coffee, so late in the afternoon?"

"I think I've answered your question—"

"Was one of the men you arrested named Jim Gum?"

My brows furrowed. "Yes. Why?"

Kincaid sat straight in his chair, moving his manacled hands from the table to rest on his lap. "He might be of use to you in finding people who got away."

I wrote the name down. When he didn't continue, I began tapping the edge of the pen on the paper.

Eventually I said, "You know that I used to be a professor at Conifer College." I met Kincaid's gaze. "I'm meeting with an old colleague at a coffee shop not too far from the college campus."

Kincaid laughed. "Good ol' Conifer. The heart of that place never seems to quit beating, does it, Dr. Grace? Though, maybe it should. Maybe it will. Very peculiar how long she's lasted, if you ask me." He stood, and the florescent light overhead cast his face into sharp shadow, once again putting in mind a hunter stalking its prey. "I want you to consider this question for next time. You said you remembered your father had a kind smile. Why? What memory is associated to that image?" He started toward the guard by the door. "Now, run along. I am sure we will be seeing each other again, very soon. Goodbye, Dr. Grace."

Giving me a slight, supercilious bow, he turned and walked through the door at the back of the room.

I stood too, watching the door as it swung shut behind the man. He walked through the outer door and I lost sight of him as he passed into the secure facility beyond.

My shoulders dropped as I let out a quiet sigh. But as glad as I was not to be under his scrutinizing gaze anymore, the answers he had left me with gnawed at me. Why on earth was knowing where I was getting coffee worth that last piece of information?

I gathered my things off the table as the sealed door behind me opened with a hiss of air, before turning and exiting the interrogation chamber.

Once on the other side, the door hissed shut behind me and my shoulders relaxed entirely. I leaned against the door for a moment, taking a deep breath.

It had been such a long week, dealing with the aftermath of dismantling the organ trafficking ring. Between interviewing Kincaid and the other traffickers, I was exhausted. As soon as I was dismissed for the day, I would be out of office until Monday, enjoying a much-needed break.

Florescent lights hummed overhead as I made my way up the grim hallway. The door ahead of me was all the way open and flush with the hallway wall. Inside was a small cubicle barely bigger than a custodial closet with a small desk, several monitors, and a control plate with a handful of knobs and buttons. A single framed picture stood beneath the rightmost monitor by the wall.

I paused at the door. "Hi, Brutus."

The small, wiry man sitting at the desk swiveled in his chair to face me, the light reflecting off his vintage glasses.

"Afternoon, Dr. Grace. Today's interview was shorter than usual, eh?"

I blew at a stray strand of hair that had fallen in my face. "Felt long enough to me."

"Nasty brute."

I nodded and gestured in his direction with my notebook. "Sorry I didn't get the chance to say hi to you last time I was here."

"It's quite alright, Dr. Grace. It's thanks to your work that that organ trafficking ring was dismantled."

"Barely." I waved his unearned compliment away. "How's your family? Your daughter doing any better?"

Brutus swiveled towards the photo on his desk. In it, Brutus sat next to a hospital bed occupied by an adolescent girl. She was covered with tubes and wires, but she gave the camera two thumbs up with a big, scraggle-tooth grin on her thin face.

"We're doing just fine, Dr. Grace. Best we can." He turned back to me, an expression of deteriorating determination on his face. "Shame that getting organs legally has so much more red tape involved. My little Annie would be right as rain if we could just find a suitable heart donor for her."

I opened my notebook's back pocket. "I've got something for her."

I handed him a small stack of stickers, all animals or rainbows with silly sayings on them.

He grinned as he shuffled through them. "She'll love these. Thank you."

I tapped the door frame. "Keep me posted, okay?"

"Yes ma'am. Have any fun plans for the weekend?"

"Heading out to Conifer, actually."

"Oh, it's nice up there. Spooky and weird. We went before Annie got admitted to the hospital. Did you know they opened a new witch shop?"

It had been months since I had been up that way, but I remembered getting a flyer in the mail about it. "I didn't know it had opened."

"Weird little place. Total tourist trap." His features wrinkled as his mouth widened into a grin. "But Annie loved the crystals they sold."

"I'll see if I can wander that way." I smiled. "Have a good weekend, Brutus."

"You're too kind, Dr. Grace." He pressed a button on the plate and the reinforced door opened for me. "See you soon."

I exited into the lobby.

After picking up my purse and down coat from the front desk, I left the building. Freezing rain blew into me, stinging my face and neck. The wind threw my hair back behind my shoulders. I threw my coat on and ran to the covered parking garage to avoid the hard droplets, cursing myself for having parked so far away.

Once I got into my car, I blasted the heat at full capacity. The air took a moment to warm. Once it did, I placed my fingers next to the air vents to coax them into thawing out.

My phone dinged and I opened it to see a number of notifications. I scrolled through them to see that I had a text waiting from my old colleague, sent to me about forty-five minutes ago.

Still on for coffee? Cynthia and I can't wait
to see you.

5

Willow

After I shot a text to Malcolm letting him know I was on my way, I dialed McCannon and pulled out of the parking lot of the east side corrections facility.

He answered on the second ring, his deep baritone rumbling through the car speakers. "Grace, I was wondering when you'd call. Meeting went shorter today, I see."

I inhaled and sighed. A few fat raindrops hit my windshield. "So everyone says."

I relayed the interview session, ending with the final tidbit he gave about Jim Gum.

"I'm not sure why knowing about my having coffee in Conifer with an old coworker was worth that," I said, "but if it helps Paxton wrap up the case with a pretty bow—"

"Then perhaps I should start sending you out on coffee runs, eh, Grace?"

I snorted as I changed lanes to leave downtown Seattle. "How's Paxton? I haven't heard from him today."

"He's due to check in anytime now." My shoulders eased at his dispassionate tone. "Without your working with Kincaid, everyone would have—" he stopped and cleared his throat. "Anyways, I'm going to have Paxton file his report before it gets handed over to the Vancouver department."

"The bodies still haven't been found then?"

"No."

"And they don't want our hel—"

"It's out of my hands, Grace." McCannon cut me off, his tone sharp. Then he sighed. "And perhaps that's for the best. Now you have a good weekend. See you bright and early Monday morning."

I nodded even though he couldn't see me. "You too, sir."

"And Grace?" McCannon's tone had turned gentle. "Don't let Paxton beat himself up over this case. What happened wasn't his fault. Baily knew the risks going into this."

Tears misted my vision, and I blinked to clear them away. "I know. But it's gonna take time for Paxton to believe that."

I ended the phone call. Soft classic rock started playing over the speakers, its beat different than that of the hail now hitting the windshield. Settling into my seat, I leaned back, resting my elbow on the door and rubbing my forehead.

It certainly wasn't Paxton's fault that Baily had died. But since Paxton had suggested that someone go undercover, he would harbor the blame. He'd been distant for the past few weeks, but I knew that it was because this case had been all consuming. It had been for everyone. It had been the biggest case in organ trafficking that the bureau had seen in a long time. Not only had a few of the organ handlers escaped, but there had been over a dozen casualties, civilians and officers alike. If that wasn't enough, the murders had all been violent, brutal, and bloody. I'd seen the crime scene photos. I had seen what they had done to Baily. Even with all my field and personal experience, this case had taken the cake.

I took several deep breaths to dissipate the images. I would be lying if I said I wasn't relieved that the Vancouver department was taking the case out of mine and Paxton's hands. Still, I wiped away the wetness on my cheeks.

Damn, did I miss Paxton. Earlier this week, he'd suggested we have a weekend away together. It wouldn't be all romance, what with the weight of this case—and Paxton still had to follow the lead from Kincaid and finish the report—but I was ready to reconnect with him. He hadn't wanted to talk about any of it. Perhaps he would be tonight.

I let the swishing of the windshield wipers lull me into a trance, thoughts washing through my brain like the streams of water off my windows.

Kincaid's question floated through my mind. What was his angle? Why was he so interested in my father?

My father. A man I truly hadn't given much thought to in years. He hadn't been a part of my life since before I could barely remember. Only with Kincaid's prompting had I remembered anything at all.

An image of a tall man bending down to pick me up formed in my mind. I had run to him and he picked me up, spinning me above his head, laughing. He'd had the best laugh.

I turned the music down and picked up my phone and opened my speech-to-text app. "Add content to text note."

The computerized female voice took a second to respond. "What file would you like to add content to?"

"Parent's file."

"Adding content to Parent's File. What would you like to add?"

"Today's date. Memory recalled today." I described the memory. "Made me feel"— I bit the tip of my tongue—"safe, warm, and loved. The recollection of the memory left me with an odd sense of loss and guilt, wrapped in apathy. To be looked into later."

I glanced at my phone screen to see the cursor moving in front of freshly typed words.

The hail continued to pound on the windows as the cityscape transformed into lush woodlands. Still dissatisfied, I shifted and started rubbing a flat hand over the lines in my corduroy pants. No matter what way I came at it, I hadn't figured out Kincaid's game.

I thought about our very first conversation. He had been secured in a plane during the transfer from Arizona to Seattle. He'd already been fascinating to me, having studied and written about him in several of my books. But he'd truly captured my attention when I turned my back on him in our first meeting.

Why you go by 'Grace,' I don't know. Peirce is a much more striking name, don't you think?

He knew my old name. No one else in the world knew my old name.

My phone rang, breaking the rhythmic drone of the road. Clicking the answer button on my steering wheel, I said, "Hey, Sinsae."

Sinsae was a good friend. We had met on a case the previous year. She and another friend, Solomon, had been instrumental in helping Paxton's niece Delphi heal from the aftermath of that same case. We had all gotten close after that.

"Willow, hey. Is now a good time?"

"Yep. Just on my way to Conifer." I took a turn off the freeway, passing a sign that read *Conifer College 15 miles.*

"Just you?"

Hearing her hesitation I quickly added, "Yeah, Paxton's going to meet me there later. He's almost tied up that trafficking case."

Sinsae whooped. "Excellent. About time, you two have been working on that damn case for weeks."

I chuckled, cheered by her enthusiasm. "Don't I know it."

"So, listen, I've been doing some digging like you asked, but the name Winnie Peirce isn't coming up in any government data bases. It's like she's been entirely erased. But as a coroner, I only have access to so many."

The back of my head thumped against the headrest. "There

aren't even documents of her case before she went into protective custody?"

"Like I said, I have limited access to information like that, but I wouldn't be surprised. Not even her wanted photo in a generic Google search comes up anymore."

"Damn." I bit my lip.

"But she's out there somewhere. These things take time."

I nodded, then remembered Sinsae couldn't see me. "You're right. I hated asking you for help with this, but it means a lot."

"Sure, I got you." She hesitated. "I still think you should tell Paxton about this, though."

Guilt pulled at the edges of my thoughts. I didn't like that this line of inquiry was shrouded in secrecy, especially from Paxton. We didn't keep secrets from each other, not since necessity had forced Paxton to reveal that he had once been married and his wife had been murdered or that I had survived and escaped a polygamist sex cult. But I also knew that he was willing to live with not knowing what had happened to Winnie Peirce and would encourage me to drop it. But I wouldn't. I had to know.

I couldn't explain why. Something about her, something other than our shared name, had pulled at me, as if we were tethered and the line had suddenly been pulled taut.

"You're right." I conceded. "I will. Soon."

Eventually. Maybe.

There was a moment of silence before Sinsae said, "Whatcha going to Conifer for anyways?"

"I'm going to have coffee with that old coworker of mine. He's finally going to introduce me to his new girlfriend."

"That's right, you told me about that. That's the guy you mentioned over Thanksgiving, right?"

"Yep, that's the one."

"And his girlfriend's the pharmacist?"

"I think so. From his descriptions of her, I got the idea she's like a homeopathic pharmacist. Makes her own tinctures and salves and stuff."

"Interesting. So you're just going down for coffee?"

"That, and Paxton and I are spending the weekend there. Just a couple days. Our phones will be off and put away, so don't be alarmed if you reach out and we don't respond."

"The lovebirds alone at last." Sinsae snickered and I blew a raspberry at her. "Hey, I gotta go. It's Book Club night and you know the one rule about Book Club."

"'Don't ever, ever be late to Book Club'." She and I chanted together then both sniggered. The weight on my chest lessened.

"Have a good time tonight."

"Will do. Chat soon. Love you, byyyyyeee!" Sinsae hung up.

The smile on my face faded. The image of that young face filled with a terrible knowledge she should never have known formed in my mind. I could still feel her chest heaving with barely controlled sobs. I never got to fulfill my promise. Never got to say goodbye.

I just needed to know that Winnie was okay.

6

Willow

Half an hour later, I pulled into downtown Conifer and found a parking spot along the main road. Local businesses, offices, and government buildings lined the pavement. In spite of the rain, locals and college students walked in hooded coats or under umbrellas, seeming intent on making the most of their Friday evening.

I sent a text to Malcolm letting him know I was here, and put on a pair of gloves.

Opening my door and planting my feet on the icy sidewalk, I shut the car door behind me and walked as fast as I could to the closest awning, slipping on the half-melted ice.

The hail had given way to rain and was coming down steadily now. Big drops pelted me as I walked towards the little coffee shop. The dark winter clouds had long since hidden the sun. Lampposts lit up the roads and sidewalks, their yellow glow reflecting off the wet pavement. A wintry breeze blew against my thin down coat, causing me to shrug my shoulders and bury my hands deeper in my pockets.

It had been many months since I had walked these streets. Giving up my teaching post at the college had been the right choice, but as I passed the different stores and businesses, I came to realize that I missed aspects of living life here. Seeing all the students walking around lifted the teacher's heart still inside me.

The clock over the bank struck four by the time the neon sign of the coffee shop came into sight. All the metal and wooden fold-up seats by the storefront were drenched and unoccupied. Olympia Coffee Roasters, written in flowing cursive on the large front window, was framed by the fog dimming the edges of the glass.

I hurried forward, my gloves making a swishing sound as I rubbed my hands together to force blood to pump through my frozen fingers. As a patron exited the café, the scent of fresh blueberry muffins wafted out behind them. Mouth watering, I was about to walk forward to enter the café when movement at the corner of my eye caught my attention.

To my left was the front of a shop I had never seen before. The window displays were filled with gems and incense beside large, hand calligraphic sale signs. Above the door swung a historically accurate 17th century sign, as if magically transported from middle age England. *The Apothecary* was written in bold black letters of Gothic print.

This must be the witch shop Brutus had referenced.

Peering through the window, I saw a familiar man leaning against the counter on one arm, drumming his fingers. His coat was dripping wet, but it was open at the front, as if he'd just popped in but had stayed longer than he'd anticipated.

A loud chiming over my head startled me as I walked in. Bells of various sizes swung and jangled above the door. Loosening my scarf from around my neck, I grinned as the man turned.

He stood up straight and grinned back at me. "Willow!"

"Hello, Malcolm."

He made to give me a hug but hesitated. The two of us had a tiny history, but I was long since past that awkward, sparkless kiss we had shared ages ago. I finished the gesture, patting his back.

"It's great to see you," I said. "I was heading to Olympia's but saw you in here."

"We should have been there by now." Malcolm raised his voice slightly over his shoulder. "But someone's running *late*."

"I'm coming, Mally." A far-off female voice came through the doorway behind the counter. "Give me two more seconds."

Malcolm shook his head, but an amused smirk lined his lips. "She really means five more minutes."

Waving my hand, I looked around, pulling my gloves off. "Wow."

Malcolm gave an approving nod. "Incredible, isn't it?"

The ground was covered in white and black checkerboard tile. Wooden beam plank paneling covered the ceiling, making the room more intimate. Gorgeous century-old wooden shelves lined every wall, the top half of the shelves being open while the lower half were all closed cabinets. A chandelier brightened most of the room along with a few wall sconces. I was half surprised to see light bulbs instead of candles, but the yellow luminescence along with the occasional flicker gave the impression of open flames. In the middle of the room was a solid oak table, covered with small baskets, each filled to the brim with gemstones. Wooden cups were filled with a hundred different scents of incense. Candles, bowls, and various animal bones covered the rest of the table. At the end of the table was a hip tall shelf overflowing with leather bound books.

Each of the shelves lining the walls were filled with jars of all sizes and hues. Some of them were filled with dried plants, but others had feathers, small bones, seeds, or items pickled in dark liquid. The jars were all labeled but as the shelves got to the front desk, the less legible they became until I realized that I was trying to read what looked to be Latin or Nordic runes.

A tingling of unease filled me, but I rolled my shoulders.

I ended my short circuit around the store at the front counter beside Malcolm. An incense fountain in the shape of a sad lion rested at the corner of the desk. Beside it was an open parchment ledger with a wooden nibbed pen resting in the middle crease. A small pot of ink sat beside the book.

"What do you think?" Malcolm asked me.

I gave a polite nod, still appraising the room. "Whimsical, archaic. Spooky."

"Precisely the atmosphere we were intending to evoke."

Malcolm and I turned. A woman dressed all in black came through the doorway behind the counter. Her strawberry blonde hair was pulled back in a messy bun. Her lavender eyes were framed by both dark smoky makeup and large circle glasses. Her lips were painted with magenta lipstick.

"Welcome to the Apothecary." Her voice was throaty, her words holding a hint of a purr. "You must be the famous Dr. Grace." She rounded the counter and grabbed my shoulders, kissing the air by both of my cheeks.

As she let me go, Malcolm stepped beside her, putting his hand on her lower back. "Willow, I would like to introduce you to Cynthia Thorne, my—"

"Lover." Cynthia finished the sentence. "It is the utmost pleasure, darling. My dear Mally has told me all about you."

Cynthia cast a glance at Malcolm, her smile taking on a more seductive note before she turned her gaze back to me.

She clasped her palms together in front of her chest. "I feel as if we are already friends."

Laughing to dispel some of the nervous energy inside, I said, "I have no doubt we will be. I'm so glad our schedules have finally aligned."

"Aligned!" Cynthia's eyes sparkled. "That is a good word. It was foretold we would meet, and at last that time is here."

"Uh," Feeling a little wrong footed, I gestured around the room. "This shop is beautiful. Is it yours?"

"In part," she said. "I am the shopkeeper. My mistress is the benefactress."

I glanced at Malcolm to see his reaction, but all I saw was amused adulation. This must be how she always spoke then. I wondered if she was naturally theatrical or if the job required her to perform.

"And speaking of my mistress"—Cynthia swooped her head around towards Malcolm, a placating smile on her face—"she came here unexpectedly today and I do admit that is why I lost track of time. She was assisting me with some projects. Currently, she's finishing an observance." Cynthia turned to me. "Then she heard I was meeting you and wanted to meet you too. I do apologize, she comes and goes as she pleases."

"That I do."

Another woman came through the door behind the counter wearing a long, flowing dress of deep lilac. Her thick silver hair cascaded down her back in princess waves. Her face was ageless, as though she could be forty or eighty. The room swelled with energy when the older woman entered, her presence demanding all attention.

"Malcolm Baldor," the woman said, walking around the counter and standing on Cynthia's other side. "A long-awaited meeting this is."

She extended her hand so that Malcolm grasped the tips of her fingers, similar to how a man would hold a woman's hand to kiss the back.

He bowed his head over her hand. "It's a pleasure to meet you, ma'am."

"You have been good to our dear Cynthia. May you continue to prove worthy of her." The woman turned to me and her eyes lit up. She inclined her head to me. "Dr. Willow Grace, a fortunate meeting this is, indeed."

This was all very strange. If this was a performance, what was it for? But something told me it wasn't one.

"I know we are unusual, but we are honored to have such a renowned doctor in our humble shop, aren't we, Cynthia?"

"I was just telling her so, Madam."

"I don't know about renowned." I flipped my hair off my neck, wincing at the sensation of a few strands still sticking to the sweat forming. "But you are very kind. Thank you...?"

"Morgana Ravenwood."

My mouth dropped open before I could stop it. "Morgana Ravenwood? Your generosity has been what's kept Conifer College running the past two decades."

"Not to mention the whole town of Conifer," Cynthia said. "There's nothing Morgana hasn't helped improve."

"When one is blessed in this life, it is only right to pay it back tenfold." Morgana inclined her head again. "Well, my children, I have kept you from your engagements far longer than I should have. I'll lock up behind you. Again, a pleasure to meet both of you."

She walked back behind the counter, before stopping in the doorway and turning back to me, her manicured palm resting on the doorframe. "Dr. Grace?"

I looked up from putting my gloves on.

"I sense you'll find her, but not in the way you would ever expect. Look out for the nine-fingered man." Then she gave a pleased nod, and she vanished.

7

Willow

I sat down at the back corner table by the window in Olympia Coffee Roasters, facing the window and rest of the room. The cramped space was filled with multiple small tables, most of which were either occupied by older couples sipping hot tea or students typing away on their laptops.

I shrugged the coat off my shoulders and tucked it over the back of my chair while Malcolm and Cynthia ordered their afternoon pick-me-ups at the register. I inhaled the buttery scent of blueberry muffins, but the comforting smell did little to ease the tension in my shoulders. What had Morgana meant about the nine-fingered man?

A gimmick? A warning? A prediction? I decided to file the interaction away for further examination later.

The interior of the windows cried with condensation, trails of tears framing the script of the coffee shop's name. I wiped some of the steam off the window with my sweater sleeve, gazing out onto the street.

The Apothecary drew my eyes with its now pitch-black windows, darker than any other store on the street. Being inside the shop had set my nerves on edge, as if my skin were on display. It had been a long time since I had felt like that.

I'm in the location of my previous life, walking the same streets, and haunting the same places. It's natural for my body to revert to my old habits of self-preservation in these environments. I am safe, I am not who I was. I have moved on and forward.

I jumped more than was warranted when my phone dinged and mentally chided myself for being too strung up. Turning the phone over, I opened it to see a text from Paxton.

> Hey honey, wrapping things up. That tip did it. Should be heading to your place in the next hour. I'll call for pizza, if you wouldn't mind picking it up?

> Of course :)

> Pineapple?

> Obviously

> You're lucky I love you

The chairs in front of me scraped across the floor as Malcolm and Cynthia went through the motions of taking off their coats and settling in.

"I do sincerely apologize for the delay," Cynthia said.

"It's no trouble," I replied. "I'm in town for a few days, so I'm in no rush to beat traffic back."

"Where ya staying?" Malcolm asked.

"My place actually."

Malcolm's eyes widened. "Really? Your little cabin in the woods?"

Another old tension—one I thought had been long put to rest—raised at the mention of my old sanctuary.

"The very same. I've been thinking of Airbnb-ing it, so figured I'd take the opportunity to check on it while I'm up here."

"That's a marvelous idea," Cynthia said. "I've managed Airbnbs before and they are such a delight. Not bad money, either."

A college-age barista with blue and yellow hair walked over with a tray and placed our drinks and pastries in front of us. After we performed the little ritual of moving plates and mugs around, I asked how the two of them met.

"It was a funny thing really," Cynthia said. "Last fall I had been invited to the school as a guest speaker for one of the classes. I was running late and I took a wrong turn. Malley and I ran into each other, literally. Papers were scattered everywhere. I ducked down to help clean up and, well," Cynthia batted her eyelashes at Malcolm.

He grinned. "I beheld the most beautiful woman lighting the hallways of Conifer."

I hid a smile behind my mug. "What class were you speaking for?"

"'Local Ceremonial Magic, History of Conifer Witchcraft'." Cynthia waggled her eyebrows at me, as if enjoying an inside joke.

"Ah, yes! Put on every fall semester by the history department. How is the dear history professor?" I asked.

We made small talk for a little while before conversation turned towards our jobs. After a few anecdotes about Malcolm's and my time together as professors at Conifer College, plus a very cryptic explanation of my job consulting for the FBI, I turned towards Cynthia.

"If you don't mind my asking," I said, "what is it that you do? From what Malcolm's told me, I was under the impression that you were a homeopathic pharmacist?"

An amused smile formed on Cynthia's lips. "Among other things, yes." Her lipstick was still flawless, despite her having drunk over half of her matcha latte. "You saw the shop I run. Filled with homeopathic pharmaceuticals, was it not?"

"I suppose, although I can't say that I recognized the majority of the items on your shelves."

"No, I suppose not. My wares serve a more... particularized clientèle base." She cast a glance at Malcom, who took a sip of his own drink. "But to give your question a better answer, darling, I am many things. A shopkeeper, an herbalist, a ritualistic curator." She took a sip, her eyes shining at me over the brim of her mug. "Or, *witch*, if you prefer."

I nodded as I folded my muffin wrapper, before dropping it on the plate. "You know, that makes far more sense than a homeopathic pharmacist."

"See, what did I tell you?" Malcolm gestured at me. "She's good with the culty stuff."

Cynthia gave Malcolm that seductive sideways glance again. "That's *occult*, dear."

Malcolm squeezed Cynthia's shoulders. "The joke was just lying on the table."

I took a sip of my mocha, wracking my brain for anything I knew about modern witchcraft. "Does that mean that you're a wiccan?"

"No," Malcolm and Cynthia said together. Malcolm continued. "I asked the same question. You can be a witch without practicing Wicca. They are not mutually inclusive of each other."

I set my mug down. "Really?"

Cynthia nodded. "Indeed, darling. It's a common misnomer. My beliefs and practices are slightly older than that of the Wicca religion."

I nudged Malcolm's coffee mug. "So, are you training to become a warlock then?"

Both Malcolm and Cynthia grimaced. "Warlock is a derogatory term, darling. Men are also referred to as witches."

I wiped my sweating hands on my pants. "Sorry, I had no idea."

"Most don't. But now you do." Cynthia's magenta smile offered a flash of warmth before she took a sip of matcha. "What did you two think of Morgana?"

"As delightful as you described," Malcolm said.

"She was very striking," I said.

Cynthia looked pleased. "It was kind of Morgana to give you that last little tidbit. About the nine-fingered man."

My muscles stiffened at the mention. I nodded and asked Cynthia how she and Morgana had started working together.

"I am still relatively new to the Conifer area, I admit." Cynthia took another sip of her matcha. "I had opened a metaphysical shop in downtown Seattle but business was sparse. Then, one day, Morgana waltzed right into my store, took one look around, and asked if I would be interested in closing down and reopening a shop in Conifer."

"Just like that?"

"Well..." Cynthia drew the word out. "What kind of entrepreneur would she be if she didn't do her research? Apparently, she felt that Conifer was in need of some more pizazz, and she wanted to bring in a business that catered to its more, uh, colorful history. When she saw that I was barely keeping afloat, she convinced me to move."

She inhaled and exhaled as she relaxed further into her seat. "And I'm so glad she did. My little Apothecary has been booming in a way I only dreamed it could back in Seattle. I don't know what I would have done without Morgana." She batted her eyelashes at Malcolm again.

The subject carried us for the next half hour, until it was time for Malcolm to head home to let his dogs out. I waved to the couple as they headed out of the shop, staying behind to order a couple cupcakes for me and Paxton.

Of all the types of people I expected Malcolm to fall for, a woman like Cynthia hadn't crossed my mind. It had been months since they had started dating so they must have been out of the 'honeymoon' stage for a while. And yet, they still looked at each other like they were in the throes of young love. What did they really have in common? Were they good for each other? I imagined a scenario of them getting married. An autumnal color scheme, with themes of bones and runes and glass. Perhaps the influential Morgana would be the officiant.

It had been neat to meet her. She had invested tons of money in different enterprises over the years, each of them more far-fetched than the last. It was in part, due to her donations, that Conifer was allowed to run as it did: more hippie and less austere. Conifer hadn't insisted on ridged structure, rather believing that creative freedom was a healthier choice, both for the individual and culture in general. Morgana had embodied that belief, always dabbling in something new. People looked up to her, so I could see her becoming certified to preside over important ceremonies. She was almost the true beating heart of Conifer.

The Apothecary drew my eyes again, and I glanced over my shoulder at its dark windows. Shaking my head, I rid myself of the images of Malcolm and Cynthia getting married. Even if they were to one day, it was really soon to be thinking about it. Too soon.

Much too soon.

... right?

8

Holt

"Hey, Holt."

I turned away from my computer, still typing as I looked over my shoulder. "Yeah, boss?"

It was evening. I was updating my report after following up on the tip given to us by Jim Gum, one of the lead operatives in the Rendezvous case. He'd been arrested the previous week. With the promise of a deal of a lesser sentence, he gave us intel that had enabled us to catch and arrest another one of the organ traffickers. My eyes burned from staring at the bright computer screen without enough sleep.

McCannon had walked over from his office, coat slung over his arm. His salt and pepper hair was still combed in place despite the five o'clock shadow around his jawline.

"How far are you from being done with that report?"

I leaned back in my chair, rubbing my eyes and face, feeling the beginnings of a beard on my face too. "I was just finishing up."

A handful of other people were packing away to leave while the night crew filed in with the same sleepy expression as those of us who came in at 5am... like I had.

McCannon half sat on my desk, looking over my shoulder. "I take it the Gum situation—"

"Panned out. Exactly as Kincaid said." I pushed my chair around to face my boss. "Gum folded. Didn't fuss or lie. Gave us the location of their hidey hole and Centry and I arrested another trafficker this afternoon. It's a wrap for Vancouver's takeover."

McCannon raised an eyebrow. "Pretty with a bow, eh?"

I grimaced. "Even ignoring the fact that there are still no bodies, it's too pretty if you ask me, sir."

"Still on about Kincaid?"

"Something doesn't sit right with me, sir." I steepled my fingers together. "I don't know what it is. Everything has gone almost too smoothly."

Barring all the deaths, of course.

"Did the autopsy reports come back?" McCannon asked.

"Yep. Look." I handed him a stack of papers. "Unusual incision patterns where the organs were removed."

McCannon rifled through the papers, a crease appearing between his eyebrows as he read. "And that means?"

"Legal operations follow a strict methodology for removing organs. This helps with limiting damage to surrounding tissue and preventing more unnecessary trauma to the body. But"—I gestured to the report—"with organ trafficking, the operators are intent on speed and concealment so naturally all legality and care for the victim goes out the window."

McCannon let out a quiet snort. "Baily certainly would have agreed."

A mix of humor and guilt stabbed me in the gut.

"You know that son of a bitch would have. This will help us should something like this ever happen again."

"God forbid."

"Amen."

McCannon chuckled without humor and stood up. "Go home, Holt. You've been working overtime for weeks. Get some rest."

"Planning on it, sir. I'm meeting Willow out in Conifer for the weekend."

McCannon nodded as he put his coat on. "You both more than deserve it. We'll see you Monday."

"Thank you, sir. Have a good weekend."

He smacked me on the back, paused as if he wanted to say more, then shook his head and left.

Rubbing my eyes, I turned back to my computer. Then I picked my phone up and sent Willow a text.

> Hey honey, wrapping things up. That tip did it. Should be heading to your place in the next hour. I'll call for pizza, if you wouldn't mind picking it up?

I set the phone down, glancing at the clock before turning back to my computer, now itching to leave.

It had been too long since I had spent quality time with Willow. Between my being assigned to the Rendezvous case and her being assigned as Kincaid's lead interrogator, we had been ships passing in the night for months.

She'd been a sport about my long hours, due in part to her patient nature, but also because she had been up to her neck with her own work on Kincaid. She hadn't shared a whole lot about it, but I suspected she was beginning a new book. Though how she was going to work through the red tape of working alongside the FBI and writing a book for the general public, I didn't know.

A few seconds later my phone buzzed.

Of course :)

Pineapple?

Obviously

I rolled my eyes, snorting.

You're lucky I love you

She sent back a smirking emoji and a red heart.

An hour later, report finished and submitted, I left the bureau. After swinging by my apartment and the store to pick up some things for the weekend, I finally got onto the highway to head to Conifer. I hadn't been out this way in months, not since we had moved Willow to the city.

Not long into the drive I came to a standstill, even though it was well past rush hour. The weekend traffic seemed worse than normal. I tapped my thumbs against the steering wheel, willing the cars ahead of me to move.

The smell of the flowers permeated the air. I reached over to the passenger side to straighten the vase, adjusting the seatbelt lower on the glass so as not to crush the bouquet of yellow tulips encased in baby's breath.

Delphi had taught me the names of over a dozen flowers, but the only ones that stuck in my mind were Willow's favorites.

I was about to pick up my phone to let her know I was on the way when it started ringing through the car speaker. Traffic started moving. I set my phone down in the cupholder with a clack and clicked the button on my steering wheel to answer the call.

"'Sup, kid."

"Heeeey, the hero lives!" my niece answered. "I was beginning to think I'd dreamt of ever having an uncle."

I chuckled, taking her sarcasm for the ribbing that it was. "Case is finished. No more selling of hearts on the black market."

"We do be loving the hearts not on the black market."

I snorted. "We do be loving that."

"I won't ask for specifics, but everything is squared away then?"

"About as squared away as it can be." Aside from about a dozen missing bodies. "Hey, wasn't your book club this afternoon? How did that go?"

"It was lovely."

She went on to tell me about her evening. I was more than happy to listen to her anecdotes about stealing Sinsae's plate of snacks and her thoughts on the book they had been reading. I'd missed her company since working on this case. She still came to spend every weekend possible with Willow and me, but between our long hours and her having started Door Dashing part-time, she'd not been able to come as frequently.

"Sounds like you had a good time," I said after she'd finished.

"Yeah, it was great."

My chest flooded with warmth. This was the most animated I'd heard her in a while.

"How're you doing, kid? Really?"

Delphi paused. "Like, how I am generally? Or how's the moving plan going? Or how I am after mom... you know."

"All of it."

She clicked her tongue. "Well, to the latter, I'm alright. I have good and bad days. Today was a good day. I've been sleeping better and I'm off the pills now entirely."

She had overdosed last fall. I raised my gaze to the sky and let out a silent breath of relief. "I'm so glad to hear that."

"As for my moving out of Marlborough, I got nothing. I was chatting with Willow about it the other day. Everything I've tried, grad school applications, job applications, reaching out to old friends, everything's fallen through. I don't know what to do. But I can't keep Door Dashing forever. I've got a dual degree in literary analysis and linguistics for heaven's sake. It's embarrassing."

Angst laced her words. I could picture her expression, her brows furrowed as she sucked on her upper teeth.

I hesitated, not wanting to say the wrong thing. Del didn't say anything either and I knew that meant she wanted my opinion.

"You know..." I said, "I was top of my class at the academy before what happened to your aunt. After she died, I was held back two class cycles. Thought I'd never catch a break."

Del made a noise to indicate she was listening.

My mouth a little dry, I continued. "I ended up graduating eighteen months later than originally planned. But if that hadn't happened, I wouldn't have gotten the assignments that eventually led me to working out of Seattle. Which means I wouldn't have ever met Willow. And it would have taken me a decade longer to pluck up the courage to reach out to you." I put my turn signal on to change lanes. "You're in your eighteen months, kid."

Del was silent for a minute longer. "Thanks, Uncle Ax."

"You're gonna be alright, kid. Both Willow and I are here for you and will help however we can."

She sighed. "I know. Thanks. So, you on the way to Conifer?"

"Yep." Traffic slowed to a crawl again. Car horns sounded in the distance behind me. "Taking forever. Evening traffic's a bitch today."

"Language!" Del's tone was filled with mock outrage. "Think of the children!"

"Excuse me, I meant to say—" and proceeded to say something I would *never* say in front of a child.

I could practically see her lifting her hand to her forehead in a mock swoon. "Oh, I'll never recover from such imprecations! What a world!"

"Once you've gotten a grip and speak like a normal person—"

"Listen, it's not *my* fault that most people have the vocabulary range of a four-year-old." She laughed. "Anyways, how are you and Willow?"

"Good, I think. I'm planning on making sure of that tonight."

"It was sweet of you to plan a getaway with her. I know she's a good sport, but I also know she's missed you."

Lord knows I've missed her too. "It's been odd. This is the first time we haven't directly worked together on a case in almost a year."

"Wow, really? I thought she'd been around longer than that."

I looked over my shoulder to check if it was safe to change lanes again. It wasn't. "Yeah. I've told you about our first case, haven't I?"

"Only a few dozen times."

"Guilty."

I picked up my now hours-old, cold coffee and took a swallow. Definitely the placebo effect, but the headache behind my eyes eased.

"So..." Del dragged the word out, her tone again losing some of its playfulness. "Do you think I'll ever get to call her 'aunt'?"

I choked on my coffee, and a few drops of liquid appeared on my dashboard. Imprecating, as Del would have described it, I picked up a napkin and began a quick wipe down.

"Like we've just established, she and I have not been dating that long, kid. It's kinda soon."

Del was silent for a moment. "Is it?"

"Del—"

"I know, I know, it's none of my business, you both have baggage, this is the first relationship either one of you has been in in over a decade, you're both learning how to be a healthy partner again, la la la, I get it."

Del took a breath. "I'm not saying that this is the right time to make a decision like that. But she gave up her teaching job to work alongside you at the FBI. You *asked* her to be your professional partner in the first place. *Because* of your baggage, you both are more compassionate and understanding of each other than other couples might be. You're a good team. It's not wrong to consider what the next step might be."

I cleared my throat, tapping my thumb against the steering wheel again. "That's a bit invasive, Delphi."

"And I'm sorry for stepping into a subject that damn well really isn't any of my business," she said. "I guess I just don't want fear to prevent you guys from anything. That's what I'm stuck in right now and well, it sucks. I know you know that."

She was silent for a few seconds before adding, "Just so we're clear, Willow didn't say, insinuate, or even breathe anything to me regarding this subject. This is purely me butting in."

I bit back the chastisement I wanted to say.

It's not that I hadn't ever thought of marrying again or even marrying Willow specifically. Of course I'd thought about it. But I was married to my job. I lived and breathed solving cases, protecting the innocent, and putting away perps. It had nothing to do with the fact that the idea of marrying again was terrifying.

But Del didn't need to know that.

Del's voice came in soft. "I'm sorry if I offended you. That really wasn't my intention."

I sighed and the anger that had surged a moment ago dissipated. "No, it's not an unreasonable question. We're just still trying to figure out how to be in a relationship again. We're not in any hurry."

"That's fair. I won't bring it up again." She let out a half-hearted chuckled. "At least, not anytime soon."

"Thanks. It's just not on our minds right now, kid."

Though now it would be on mine.

9

Willow

IT WAS APPROACHING SIX NOW AND THE CAFÉ WAS ALMOST empty. The last of the college students were packing up their laptops and schoolbooks. Two older women walked out of the shop holding hands.

As I perused the eclectic art on the side wall, the one of a vaseful of lilies caught my eye. Though the different shades on the petals and vase were painted in neon colors, the painting itself was hyper realistic. It reminded me of Delphi, Paxton's niece. She was steady, down-to-earth young woman with a streak of vibrancy in her that was a pleasure to witness.

After a decade of separation, she and Paxton had taken a shot at reforming their relationship. I could only be grateful that she had taken my relationship with her uncle in stride, accepting me into her little family circle—one that had only shrunk with the murder of her mother. The foundation of mine and Paxton's relationship with her had been laid over the months since the case that had thrown us all together and it had solidified after her overdose scare the previous fall. I thought about the last time I had talked to her, a phone call we'd had earlier that week. I wasn't yet used to the maternal warmth that had filled me when I had looked up from the notes on my counter and saw her caller ID light up my phone.

I had answered the call immediately. "Hey Delphi."

"Willow, hey. You busy?"

"A bit, but I could use a break," I'd said, closing my notebook. "What's up?"

"Same actually." She paused. "I just got another college rejection letter."

I tsked. "Aww, Del, I'm sorry."

"Yeah, me too. Second one this week. And I've applied to, like, a gazillion jobs and no one's gotten back to me. Guess I'm just bummed out."

"I would be too. That really stinks. How's the house situation going?"

"That's going alright. I've finished going through everything and have put Mom's house on the market. I don't think it'll take too long to sell. Once it does, I'll have the money to pay for college, if they'd just accept my application." Her tone was heavy with rejection-exasperation fatigue.

"I know. You'll find something, you just gotta keep trying."

She snorted.

I chuckled. "I always hated that advice too. But something will stick. Your uncle and I have our ears to the ground for you."

A draft of air hit me as the door opened, pulling my attention back to the present. A young woman in a thick coat and hiking boots walked up to the counter.

"Pick-up for Caroline?"

I turned to look at the young woman fully. I'd had a student named Caroline. You weren't supposed to have favorites as a teacher, but she was one of mine. The dual-colored hair barista handed the woman a paper bag over the counter.

Caroline's eyes landed on me and she stopped short. "Professor Grace?"

I stepped toward her, my mouth widening into a grin. "Caroline!"

She ran forward and threw her arms around me, the food bag swinging around and hitting us both on the side.

She dropped the bag on the table and sat down in the vacated seat across from me. "How are you? What are you doing back here?"

"I was actually just meeting with Professor Baldor for coffee," I told her.

Caroline gasped. "Does this mean you're coming back? Did he convince you to come back?"

I let out a sad chuckle. "No. I've decided to stay on with my new job."

Caroline groaned but nodded. "Can't blame me for hoping."

After exchanging news from when we had last seen one another, a conversation I had had with Delphi the first time I met her popped into my head.

"Wait, you're the cult expert lady?" Delphi's cheeks had bloomed into a rosy blush. "I'm sorry, I didn't mean for that to sound so callously blasé."

I had smiled, amused by the assessment. "No, you're right. I am the cult expert lady."

"One of my friends took your class at Conifer College. Her name's Caroline?"

I looked at Caroline and an idea popped in my head.

"Do you know a Delphi Augur?" I asked.

Caroline's face lit up. "Del? She and I were good friends growing up."

"Would you believe that she's my partner's niece?"

"You mean you and that FBI agent actually hit it off? That's awesome! Small world!" Caroline gave the table a staccato smack.

"She and I went to school together before— " Caroline's cheeks turned red. "Before she had some family stuff happen."

"You mean her mom's murder?"

"What?" Caroline mouth dropped open. "No, I was talking about her dad! What—oh my gosh—"

I grabbed Caroline's hand, putting a mental pin in the comment about Del's dad. "I'm sorry to have dumped that on you."

I gave her a brief rundown of what had happened last fall, curious she hadn't already heard about it from local news.

Caroline swore. "That's terrible. Is she okay? It's been a while since she and I chatted, but I hadn't realized it was *that* long."

"She's doing the best she can," I said. "But it might do her some good to hear from an old friend."

"Absolutely, I'll reach out to her. Is there anything else I can do?"

I thought for a moment. "She's trying to get out of Dodge, but she's having a hard time figuring out her next steps. Everything she's tried has fallen through. Do you maybe know if anyone's looking to hire?"

Caroline scrunched her brow. "You know... this might be farfetched." She bit her lip. "But I've got some friends up in Alaska that own a summer camp. They're looking for employees during the rest of the year to help maintain the grounds. Maybe she'd be interested?"

I blew out a breath of air and squeezed her hand. "Caroline, there's a reason you were my favorite student."

"Ma'am!" The dual hair color barista ran up to the table, holding a white cardboard box. "Your red velvet cupcakes. I totally forgot about them, I'm sorry. I saw you eying the salted caramel too, so I put two of those in there for you to make up for the wait."

I took the box, heart swelling at the unexpected kindness. "You didn't have to do that."

The barista's shoulders relaxed at my words. "We would have had to toss them tomorrow morning anyways."

"Thank you"—I squinted at her name tag—"Suza, that's so kind of you."

She shrugged. "Sure thing. Also, um, the shop will be closing in five."

Both Caroline and I checked the time, exclaimed, then stood.

We walked out of the café together and parted ways on the sidewalk, promising to keep in touch.

I waved to her and made my way to my car.

As I slid inside, my phone chimed. I pulled it out to see Paxton's message.

Hey, forgot to text you. I'm headed your way now. About forty minutes out.

Sweet, I'm heading to get pizza now. See you soon <3

Throwing my phone into the passenger seat, I put the car into gear to head to the pizzeria before heading to my old home.

The home I hadn't seen in months.

I pulled up the long, wooded driveway and parked in my usual spot. A familiar sense of comfort and foreboding entered my shoulders. I pushed my seat back and pulled my legs up so that my knees and shins were resting at an angle against the steering wheel. The soft beat of the folk music played at a low volume. I nodded my head in rhythm, watching the rain pelt my windshield with sharp, staccato plunks.

Steam from the pizza wafted through the boxes, the smell of garlic butter making my mouth water. I checked my watch and guessed that Paxton would be pulling up in the next fifteen minutes.

My eyes traced the outside of the house, a shadow forming in the growing darkness. It was the same as it had been when I left some six months ago. The cameras and lights were still mounted in places you could only see if you knew where to look.

A shiver skated up my arm and I had to laugh at myself.

My life was nothing but fear living here. Even now, I still felt uneasy and I hadn't been here in months. I had lived in one of the most fortified places a woman with limited money could buy and I rarely left its safety.

I pressed my head back into the head rest, hugging my arms around my knees.

I had been afraid of my old life finding me. But even after my false first husband who had married me, as a minor, under fanatical and illegal means had been killed, my fears of being found out hadn't dissipated. The fears of discovery had then turned into fears of being known. Of letting someone in. Which only proved what I had long since considered—that this safe haven was a different kind of prison, but this time of my own making.

I had been imprisoned in many ways in my life, from physically locked behind bars to trapped behind a cult leader's regime.

Safety had been, above all, what I'd valued. I still did. I couldn't function if I didn't feel sure of solid ground, in at least one area of my life. It used to be this cabin.

Now it was Paxton.

A deep breath rose within me at the thought of getting to be with him, alone, unencumbered by work or worry for the first time in weeks. Serenity pushed the foreboding away.

Paxton was my home. He was safety, far more than this little cabin had been for a decade of my life. He was my family.

I blinked, my eyes suddenly watery.

I hadn't had a family in years. I tried to remember a time when I had.

Back in Fountain of Faith, the cult I had escaped over a decade ago, I'd had my old friends, Bethany and Tom, who were now living in Arizona. Before that, my mother. The smell of cigarettes filled my nose at the thought of her, an ache filled my chest. I remembered that smell more than I remembered her face.

Where had my father been?

I wracked my brain, but I could not produce a single image nor memory beyond what I had said to Kincaid earlier in the day. Tall. A kind smile. Blue or hazel eyes. As I dwelt on it, the smell of pine needles came to mind.

Had I really had a father? Or were any memories just the conjuring of a lonely child, desperate for protection I'd never known?

Light caught my review mirror. I stiffened, pressing completely back into my seat as a car pulled into the driveway.

10

Willow

Paxton and I sat together on my old couch, watching the fire he had lit in the fireplace. He was wrapped around me, rubbing his hands up and down my arm and shoulder, resting his cheek on top of my head. I tucked my feet under me as I nestled into his chest, admiring the bouquet of flowers Paxton had brought me, now sitting on the kitchen counter next to the half empty box of cupcakes.

Folk music emanated from an old CD player. Over the soft guitar riffs, I was telling him of my chance meeting with Caroline and her promise of reaching out to Del.

"I think this might be a good thing for her," I said. "Even if it doesn't pan out, hearing from an old friend would cheer anyone up."

Paxton grunted, adjusting his feet on the old coffee table. He bumped the empty pizza box resting on the edge of the table and it fell to the floor. We sat for a few more minutes, the hum of the generators filling the silence. Since the cabin was off grid, we had to turn the generators on to provide electricity, but I had lit the candles I brought anyways. Between that and the fireplace, the open floor plan was basked in warm, flickering light.

I looked up at Paxton, keeping my head on his chest. "Still unhappy about her leaving?"

"A decade of wasted time." Paxton shook his head. "Just got her back and losing her already."

"You're not going to lose her. *She* won't let that happen any more than you will."

"I'm responsible for her, Willow." Paxton kept rubbing my arm. "She's got no other family watching her back. After everything that's happened over the last few months, her mom, her job—"

"Are not your fault."

"No." Paxton conceded, but his hand began to move faster up my arm. "But she's a kid. What if, wherever she goes, whether it's Alaska or Timbuktu, she falls flat on her face and I'm not there to help her?"

I sat up, gently pushing his hand away and holding it in my own. His eyes widened. "First of all, you're rubbing me raw. Second, Delphi is *not* a kid. She's trying to sell her first *house* for heaven's sake. Neither you nor I had any real estate to sell when we were her age. She's graduated college and has been on her own for a few years. She's not inexperienced in adulthood."

Paxton released a breath. "I know. You're right. I just want to help her, be a part of her new life, wherever that is."

"And we *will*," I told him, rubbing my thumb over the back of his hand. "But we have to let her figure it out. All we can do is support her and love her and give her a leg up where we can."

A glimmer of amusement came into Paxton's expression. "Very parental of you."

I threw my hands up. "Guilty."

"Delphi thinks we should get married."

My face warmed by twenty degrees, heart now pounding against my ribs. "Really?"

Paxton pulled his hand out of mine and sat up straighter too. He gave me a searching look. "I told her it was a bit soon for that conversation."

I cleared my throat. "What did she say to that?"

"Essentially that you and I have already done big things for each other and despite our baggage, we are a great team and—" He huffed in amusement, rubbing a palm against the back of his neck. "Basically, we should get on with it."

I couldn't help but start laughing.

Paxton also chuckled, still eying me.

Taking his hand again and squeezing it, I said, "I don't want this to be a hitch or a point of contention so I'll say that I am not opposed to the idea." I took a deep breath, hoping he hadn't noticed my hands starting to sweat. "But we don't have to talk about it right this second."

Paxton relaxed, his shoulders easing. "That's exactly what I was thinking. Not opposed, but let's shelve it for later."

I nodded. "We're good?"

He nodded back. "We're good." Then he pulled me to him and wrapped his arms around me again. My heartbeat slowed and my hands stopped sweating.

"How was your time with Malcolm?" he asked.

"It was really nice. Got to jaunt down memory lane. I got to meet a real live witch today."

"What?" Paxton pulled away enough for me to see one of his eyebrows raised to his hairline.

I chuckled. "Yeah, his girlfriend Cynthia, is a real, self-proclaimed witch. Runs an actual apothecary across the street from the coffeeshop we met at."

"No kidding. She perform any spells for you?" He gave me a look of mock concern. "Or *on* you?"

I knew Paxton was ribbing me, but Morgana's exhortation about the nine-fingered man came to the forefront of my mind again. "Well, she didn't, no."

"Well, good." Paxton squeezed my shoulders. "You're perfect the way you are, so I'd hate for some hocus pocus to change that."

I couldn't help but laugh. "Not one for the hocus pocus, huh?"

Paxton snorted. "Never done a damn thing to help law enforcement, I'll tell you that."

"Riiight, and your grumpy attitude has?"

Paxton huffed in mock outrage and dug his fingers into my side.

Once I fought off his tickling I collapsed back into his arms, breathless and grinning. "I've missed you," I whispered.

Paxton kissed the top of my head. "I've missed you too, love."

"I'm proud of you by the way. For everything you've done lately."

Paxton shifted, letting out another huff. "I don't deserve that, Willow. Not with everything that happened."

"You mean with your team managing to shut down an organ trafficking ring?"

"While losing another dozen civilians and an agent in the process?"

"It wasn't your fault."

"So everyone keeps saying."

"Paxton."

He turned his eyes to mine, his gaze sharp but open. His bitterness wasn't directed at me, but himself.

"Whenever things don't go the way you plan or when accidents happen or things fly outside of your control, you blame yourself. That isn't healthy, nor is it *ever* true. You need to learn how to forgive yourself."

Paxton pulled away from me while holding my shoulder, still holding my gaze. "How, Willow? How am I supposed to do that?"

I placed my palm on his cheek. "By putting the blame where it belongs, for one thing. On the people who are responsible."

"I may not have wielded the tool that killed Baily, but I might as well have. If I'd just prepared him better for the dangers he'd be facing. He didn't have enough intel. If I hadn't suggested—"

"Then someone else would have made the suggestion. Would you ever say McCannon was to blame had *he* been the one to suggest someone go undercover?" I gestured to myself. "Or me?"

His eyes jumped between both of mine. "That's different."

"It really isn't." I nuzzled into his side again. "I can't get rid of your guilt. But I can help you work through it. You just gotta listen to me."

"Just my luck I fall in love with a psychologist."

I laughed.

"We wouldn't have been able to do any of it without you," he said, lips moving against my hair. "Your work with Kincaid has been insurmountably helpful."

I shrugged. "Just doing my part."

Paxton started rubbing my shoulder again, his touch a gentle caress. "Is he still asking about your dad?"

"Yeah." A weight lowered onto me again at the recollection of the conversation I had had with Kincaid earlier that day. "I can't figure out his angle. What good does knowing about my past do him?

"I mean, you are a very interesting person. *I* want to know everything about you."

"Touché. I wrote some more notes down after today's meeting, though. I'll look back at it later."

"That's good." Paxton gazed around the living room. "You know, it's kinda crazy."

"What is?"

"Us being here together. To think that this is where we would end up when I knocked on your door that night."

I looked around the room, remembering that night. How scared I had been to see a strange man at my door. How, even through my unease, I had noticed he was handsome. Not long after, I observed that he was kind. He was good with children, excellent at his job, and intent on righting the wrongs in the world. He wasn't perfect, but he was a good man.

"You're right," I said. "And now we're talking like parents, eschewing marriage, and discussing trauma."

Paxton chuckled. "A very romantic spin on that thought there, love."

"Learned from the best."

And he leaned down to kiss me, sweet and slow.

We went to bed shortly after. The rest of the weekend together was wonderful, filled with coffee on the porch, hikes around the area, and evenings spent by the fire.

At the end, Paxton kissed me goodbye, leaving my stomach warm and fluttering. He rumbled out of the driveway while I finished packing up my own car before heading back to Seattle. I turned my phone on for the first time in days, my mind clear from the digital detox.

Once I was out of the woods and back to better cellular connection, my phone started dinging with notifications.

I stopped at a stop sign and picked it up, swiping the social media, weather, and email notifications away. The last to pop up was the title of a news article that had my skin prickling with chills.

BELOVED PHILANTROPIST PASSES ON: CONIFER MOURNS THE LOSS OF MORGANA RAVENWOOD

11

Selena

Selena watched as her grandmother was lowered into her grave.

The smell of petrichor and freshly dug earth permeated the air, lonely and sad. Rain sprinkled the grass and speckled the large monument her grandmother had chosen as the marker for her corpse's final resting place. Tears leaked from the life-size stone lion at the top of the monument, as if the very elements of the world lamented the loss of so great a woman.

Perhaps they did.

Her grandmother's funeral and wake had taken place earlier that day. Hundreds of attendees. Speeches. The best food and wine. Her grandmother would have been very well pleased.

Now, only the chosen few were present for the committal service.

Words were spoken over her grandmother's corpse hidden behind a lid of marked and sacred wood. The owner of the voice, the local priest, soon left, leaving behind a small group of people, all in white, around the grave.

Selena took in the box containing what was left of her grand-mother, her eyes tracing the sacred symbols embellishing the box. Symbols of protection and preservation.

Now her grandmother could never be hurt again. All the cares the great woman had had now rested on the shoulders of others. Namely Selena's. A single tear fell down her cheek, blending with the mist falling from the sky.

Her very bones felt like lead weights. She was so tired.

The strongest among them pushed the stone slab over her grand-mother's coffin. Stone scrapped against itself as the lid jutted into place, the sound ripping through the air. The silence afterward over-whelmed the small crowd.

A small figure came up beside her and put a hand on her forearm. Selena stiffened, recognizing the light, airy perfume of the wearer, a contrast to her own rich, intoxicating scent. She turned to assess the small woman. Dressed in white, head covered in a dark, partial veil, Celeste Black was the image of heavenly beauty. The only mar were her red eyes, raw at the corners from crying.

"Are you up for attending the summit?" she asked Selena. "They're all waiting for you."

Celeste was always so gentle. So compassionate. So performative.

Selena despised her for it.

Shrinking away from Celeste's hand, Selena turned around, assessing the dozen people lingering around the grave. The only ones who should be there. Her grandmother's chosen followers. They all were now looking at Selena, waiting. Some looked at her with broken hearts. Others looked at her with narrowed eyes, watching. Still others looked troubled. Selena turned back to Celeste and nodded.

As if under a spell, the group of people, men and woman alike, all turned and started walking into the woods.

Selena and Celeste made up the rear of the party. Selena sensed Celeste look behind them, checking for watchers.

There were none, obviously. They all would have known.

For some time they walked through the trees, making their way to a special place in the forest, far away from prying eyes or ears. Along the way, they passed the forbidden gate. Selena paused to peer at it.

Her grandmother had never allowed her or any of her followers to pass through the gate. Anywhere on the estate they could roam, frolic, forage, practice, do anything they'd like *except* pass through the gate. Selena walked up to it, looking past the welded metal to the dirt road behind. She squinted at the ruts in the road, as if a vehicle had recently passed through.

"Selena?" Celeste's voice broke her thoughts. She stood waiting a few yards ahead.

Selena continued walking. As she caught up with Celeste, she looked over her shoulder, but they had rounded a bend. The gate was lost from sight.

Eventually, they came to a clearing deep in the woods, the ground bare of anything, even leaves. The open space was encompassed like a tomb, the forest ceiling and walls of greenery curved so that the open space was a perfect sphere. It was dark like twilight, despite the afternoon light trying to peek through the canopy above. Rain pattered against the forest floor, churning the mulch outside the sphere. A light breeze whistled through the branches, creating a cacophony of crepitation.

The people moved to stand in a circle. One space was left open, at the top of the circle, due north. All stood a foot apart from one another and waited. The air was tense with unspoken questions.

"What is to be done now?" A voice in the circle asked.

Selena looked around. She hadn't seen who had spoken but she knew it to be the woman who worked in the shop her grandmother had funded.

"That which is expected of us," Celeste responded. "What else?"

"But should we follow through with those wishes? When her life ended so abruptly?"

"Her death was deemed by natural causes." Another voice said.

"There is no reason not to follow through with our matriarch's wishes and our traditions."

The circle chanted, "Earth bless the matriarch."

A figure stepped forward, hands raised in ceremony above his head. "That leaves the foreseen candidates for us to consider," the Keeper of Knowledge said. "After our allotted days of mourning, we will hold a conclave to decide who is best suited to lead us."

Celeste lowered her head and dull satisfaction seeped into Selena's chest. An easy win. A simple win. She knew what her grandmother would have wanted.

"Selena and Celeste," the Keeper of Knowledge said, "you knew her best. May her spirit find rest in the knowledge that you will carry on her legacy, no matter who or what comes next."

Both Selena and Celeste inclined their heads to the speaker. Celeste then threw her arms out, as if to embrace the whole group.

"Start a bonfire," she said. "We all know how much our matriarch loved to dance. Let us celebrate her life with the beauty and power of movement."

The tension in the air snapped as, one by one, each member nodded. Wood appeared and they all began erecting it into a large pile in the center of the clearing. In mere moments a bonfire scorched the forest floor, illuminating the trees surrounding them. Music echoed through the clearing and they all began dancing.

And oh, what a sight it was to see, their dancing. The chanting, the flickering of the flames, the sensuous movement, thrusting, grinding, spinning, twirling, intoxicating.

Their celebration of their dead matriarch was a wonder to behold. The very air was filled with the breath and scent of their sorrow and commemoration.

After a time, Selena stood apart from the others, watching. Grief filled her heart. She hadn't even gotten to say goodbye, to ask the wisest woman she had ever known one last question.

Celeste came up beside her. For a while the two of them didn't speak, their eyes remaining on the dancers' silhouettes.

"How did it happen?"

Selena almost didn't hear Celeste over the sound of the music. She didn't have to answer. She owed Celeste nothing. But she knew how much her grandmother cared for the small woman. For Selena's rival. As much as she hated their rivalry, she respected her grandmother more.

"I found her lying on the floor, head right beside the stone corner of the fireplace in her office." She kept her eyes fixed on the bonfire in the middle of the writhing couples. "I must have found her right after it happened. She was still... warm."

"Did the revival rite not do anyth—"

"You think I wouldn't have said something if it had?" Selena snapped, turning to look at the woman. "About my own grandmother?"

Flickering shadows and light danced across Celeste's face. "I was only asking."

"It was an accident," Selena said, bitterness leaving her cheeks wet. "A simple, stupid, *pointless* accident." The full weight of her loss crashed into her, leaving her knees buckling.

A single tear fell down Celeste's face. "I'm so sorry, Selena."

And that time, Celeste's words were a comfort, however small. "As am I."

After another few minutes, Celeste said, "The Keeper of Knowledge will record this legacy."

Selena nodded.

Celeste's voice deepened. "May the best one of us win the Matriarchy."

12

Some weeks later...

Willow

PAXTON PULLED UP TO THE POLICE TAPE, THE SPRING BREEZE already blowing away the cloud of dust kicked up from the tires. Two men in police uniforms watched as we drove up to the pocket of openness in the middle of the woods.

One officer stood poker straight, pressed uniform and baby face cheeks had all the tell-tale markings of a rookie. I noted the badge on the other's belt as he approached the car and nodded to me through my side window. I rolled it down.

The sun had come out in full force, causing the man to squint his baby blue eyes, his handlebar mustache waxed stiff against the breeze.

I glanced at Paxton, trying to envision him with a mustache. For the record, I couldn't. The officer rested his hands on the window edge and gave us both a once-over. "Dr. Grace? Agent Holt?"

We nodded.

"I'm Sheriff Lance, with me is Officer Davis. Park over there"—he waved to a spot along the side of the road, behind several other police vehicles—"and I'll show you the crime scene."

He took a step back as Paxton pulled forward to follow his instructions.

"Shame we don't get to work with ol' Howie again," Paxton said. Deputy Sheriff Howie had worked with us on our first case together.

I nodded as I unbuckled my seatbelt. "We're not in the same county, though we aren't far from the college grounds."

I stepped out of the car, basking in the warmth of the sunlight amidst the cool spring breeze. The road cut through the area, with woods lining the lane on the west side of the road and the ground opening out on the west after the drainage ditch. Sheriff Lance and the other officer stood atop a strip of dirt that blocked the ditch, wide enough for a vehicle to drive over. Behind them, a small meadow was blocked off by police tape. More officers bent down to stick flags in the grass or photograph the scene, their movements rigid and hastened.

Paxton and I made our way toward the officers, passing through the clumps of trees dotting the stretch of tall, brown grass. Less than a handful of miles from here was Conifer's downtown area, though you would never know it by the surrounding wilderness. In another direction, a few miles further out, was the edge of the Conifer College grounds.

Lance nodded at us, opting out of shaking hands as he snapped on a pair of latex gloves.

"We appreciate you coming out here on such short notice," Lance said to us. "We took one look at the scene and knew we needed to bring in the Feds. Have you read over the report?"

"We read it on the way down," Paxton replied.

My stomach clenched at Paxton's words. It hadn't been easy

reading through the report. Paxton flashed me a quick, knowing look, his eyes filled with disquiet. Lance nodded and Davis handed each of us our own pair of gloves. We pulled them on, and Lance held the tape up for us to walk under, then led the way down a soft decline into the meadow. Our shoes squelched against the ground's muddy surface. Water gushed into my shoes, making my socks soggy.

"We've never seen something like this before," Lance told us over his shoulder. "We're hoping that between your field experience"— he nodded to Paxton— "and your occult expertise, Dr. Grace, that you'll be able to provide us some fast answers. We haven't been able to identify the body yet, but I wouldn't be surprised if it's one of those kids from Conifer College."

Though I had dived into the occult in my research, my area of expertise was cult psychology and victimology. However, I decided not to remind the sheriff of that. Instead, I focused on keeping my balance as we crossed the uneven, soggy ground and keeping my fears at bay. Apprehension prickled up my spine, sending goosebumps up and down my arms despite the unseasonable warmth. The report had indicated that the victim was young and likely college-aged. I didn't know how I would react if it turned out to be one of my old students. We walked a hundred more yards and came up to the circle of flags. Two officers—one who had been taking pictures and another who had been putting down flags—were whispering to each other. We passed them, and I turned my gaze to the ground.

In the middle of the grassy field was a small mound of dry dirt. A young man lay on his back, his arms spread in a T. Dark hair, cropped close to the scalp, either late high school or early college age and pearly white skin, almost transparent as if all the blood had drained from him. He was completely naked.

His eyes were closed and face relaxed as if in sleep, if it weren't for the gaping hole in his chest. A cavity on the left side of the chest, right where his heart should have been, was open to the elements. Blood pooled in the exposed chest cavity. Around his body, lovingly arranged, were bright white lilies. The white was so stark that every-thing around it looked dim and gray in comparison. Surrounding the body in a perfect circle were symbols etched deep into the dirt.

Relief and guilt flooded through me. Paxton pressed a covert hand on my lower back and I gave him a tiny headshake. I didn't recognize the young man.

"I want this perimeter widened," Lance called out and several of the officers started moving. "Have the lilies been processed into evidence?"

One officer called out an affirmative. Lance nodded and invited Paxton and me to begin our investigation.

Careful not to mar the characters on the ground, Paxton stepped closer to the body and squatted down. I bent down to observe the symbols more closely. A sickly-sweet smell hit me hard enough to make me gag. The smell of lilies mixed with something sharper, like a chemical or medicine. Then something rich and hazy, almost like a perfume.

Paxton traced the ground with the very tip of his finger. "He can't have died here."

"Why?" Lance asked, his arms folded over his chest.

Paxton looked up at the other man. "Where's the blood?"

Turning back to the body, he scrutinized the open chest wound. "Whoever did this, knew how to do it." He pointed at the chest opening. "You see how precise the opening is? See how—"

"The ribs have been spread apart?" Lance interrupted, nodding. "We noted that. Perhaps a surgeon or medical professional?"

Paxton pulled his notebook and pen from his pocket and started taking notes. He put the tip of his pen between his teeth and muttered, "I've seen this before."

Lance glanced down at me, but I quirked my shoulder in shared ignorance. He asked, "What's that, Agent Holt?"

Paxton stood up and stepped over the symbols on the ground to stand next to Lance. "How long's he been dead?"

"Medical examiner hasn't made it in yet, so we can't be sure. Given that rigor mortis hasn't fully set in, my guess is he's been here since early this morning."

"Who found the body?" I asked.

"It was actually an anonymous phone call. Answered it myself. Male with a British accent said we needed to come and check out a body in Innocence Field."

Paxton and I shared a glance before he asked, "Find any evidence? Any weapon, footprint?"

Lance waved an officer over and had her hand Paxton a plastic bag containing a piece of paper. "This was underneath the vic's head."

I looked over Paxton's shoulder. The small piece of paper had lateral and horizontal creases in it. It had been folded in half and in half again. The note on it had been written in bold, flowing handwriting.

Paxton read aloud, "'*Listen to her*'." He looked back up at Lance. "Who's 'her'?"

"I'd love to know the answer to that, too," Lance said. "We're searching, but we haven't found anything else."

"There's gotta be something," Paxton said. "I mean, how did the perpetrator even get the body out here?"

Lance gestured to the other officers. "Murphy!"

The officer who had been taking pictures turned to his commanding officer and approached us. "Sir?"

"This is Special Agent Holt and Dr. Willow Grace."

Paxton and I nodded at the young officer, barely older than the victim.

"Tell 'em what you told me earlier."

Murphy turned his whole body to Lance, as if trying to shield himself from the corpse. He cast the briefest glance in the body's direction and blanched before clearing his throat. "Sir, are you sure?"

"Yes," Lance said.

Murphy swallowed and fiddled with the camera strap around his neck. "It's just that—" He stopped, a flush creeping up his glistening face. He glanced at the body again. "Well, me and some of the other guys were wondering if maybe the... the witches did this."

13

Willow

Paxton stared at the young officer, his voice laced with amused skepticism. "You think witches did this."

"It's not as far-fetched as it sounds," I said. "There is actually history of witchcraft in the area. One of the history classes they offer at the college is all about the local history of witches and witchcraft."

Murphy shuffled his feet. "The kid's been found on Ravenwood Estate. So..." He cleared his throat, giving the ground a significant look.

"Ravenwood?" I asked. "As in Morgana Ravenwood?"

Murphy nodded. "The very same."

Paxton grunted. "So... what does being on the Ravenwood Estate have to do with this?"

Murphy flushed. "Ah, well... it's just that..."

"Spit it out, Murph," Lance said, not unkindly. "We're listening to all hypotheses at the moment."

Murphy nodded and cleared his throat again. "Back in the day, the Ravenwood Estate was known as the meeting grounds for all local witches. And Morgana Ravenwood's been around forever. Almost unnaturally long, if you believe the rumors. But then you add those... those symbols?" Murphy pointed to the characters around the body. "It speaks for itself, if you ask me."

Paxton hid a snort behind a loud sniff, rubbing his nose as if allergies were bothering him. I, on the other hand, was intrigued. In all my years living outside of Conifer, I had never known the witchcraft rumors to be so prevalent. Sure, I had heard some rumors about Morgana's supposed unnaturally long life and I had enjoyed sitting in on some of the witchcraft history lectures the college offered on the subject, but beyond that I hadn't thought much of it.

"I wanted to ask you your thoughts on those symbols, Dr. Grace," Lance said. "Can you offer any intel about them?"

I turned and stooped next to the symbols again. A circle framed three symbols, the markings inside each of them unique. The carvings were etched deep enough into the soil that liquid had filled them.

I stuck a finger into one of the groves and brown red liquid stained my fingertip.

"This whole set up is quite ritualistic," I said, pulling the glove off. "Everything is set up in meticulous detail. The way the body's laying, the carved and bloody symbols, the way his heart was removed." I looked back at the men. "The person who did this was orderly and clearly had the time to set things up."

Lance nodded. "What else?"

"Why the lilies?" I looked back at the flowers surrounding the body, thinking. "The name of this place is 'Innocence Field', right? Lilies are often connected to the concept of innocence. I suspect that might be of significance."

"Or," Paxton said, "it's a diversion."

Lance's gaze narrowed. "What do you mean?"

"Know anything about the Rendezvous case?"

"Terrible business." He glanced between us. "That was you two, right?"

I stood and nodded. Paxton pointed to the body. "That chest wound? That's exactly like what we found working that case." Paxton's shoulders tensed. "I'll grant it's too soon to tell, but if this is another sect of that same trafficking ring but they'd want to divert us with all these"—he gestured around us—"theatrics."

"That's a hell of a lot of work for the traffickers." I bit my lip, glancing back at the body. "Why bother? Why bring the body out here in the first place?"

Murphy nodded at me. "Witches have something to do with this, I guarantee it."

Paxton raised a hand, pen tucked between his fingers. "I'm just saying I'm not sold on anything yet."

Lance dismissed Murphy before saying to Paxton, "Your hypothesis seems far-fetched. I don't think—"

A car door slammed across the meadow. A petite woman ducked under the police tape and ran towards us.

"Hey!" Her tone was furious.

"Ma'am! This is police business—" Officer Davis ran after her, holding onto his hat.

"Terran, this is private property, how dare you—"

The woman ran up to Lance, about to stick a finger into his face when she caught sight of the body behind us and froze. Her lovely, porcelain face flushed and tears formed in her green eyes.

"Ms. Black," Lance said calmly, as if it wasn't unusual for this petite woman to show up on crime scenes uninvited. His eyes narrowed as he watched her absorb the scene behind us. "Do you know him?"

She didn't respond.

I looked her over, admiring her Rosie the Riveter hairstyle. She was wearing all black, from her head scarf to her shoes. Maybe the dark fabric hid stains well, but there wasn't a fleck of mud or dead grass on her shoes or the hems of her trousers. Odd.

Lance raised his eyebrows. "Ms. Black?"

Ms. Black sucked in a quick breath and glanced up at Lance before turning her gaze to Paxton and me.

"I do seem to have stuck my foot in it this time," she said, her flush deepening. "Yes, I knew him."

"Let's go back to the vehicles," Lance said, sweeping one hand out and putting his other close to her back to guide her forward.

She nodded and the two of them headed back up to the police tape.

"Betcha ten bucks that they—" Paxton whispered a suggestive hypothesis in my ear as we followed the two.

I suppressed a snort and smacked his arm. "We are at a crime scene, be serious."

We came up to the police tape across the entrance and Paxton held it up for me. Lance's mouth was in a line almost hidden under his mustache in an expression like, *sorry about this.* Ms. Black held herself, rubbing her thumbs against her arms.

"Ms. Black, this is Special Agent Holt and Dr. Willow Grace," Lance said. Ms. Black eyes snapped between us when Lance said our names. "This is Ms. Celeste Black, chairwoman of the Conifer town's council."

Paxton and I both acknowledged the introduction.

"What an honor. I am delighted to meet you." She reached out and shook both of our hands, her manicured grip strong.

She was much calmer now, her eyes now dry and face returning to pure porcelain. "Please allow me to explain myself. I am one of the executors of the Ravenwood Estate. Innocence Field is part of the Ravenwood Estate. That's why I walked past the police tape. Ever since Morgana passed—" her voice broke on the name. She allowed herself a moment to look away and swallow before continuing. "We've had so many trespassers. It's not a good excuse, but I thought that's what this was. Then I saw Vyvan." She shook her head. "I apologize for my interference."

Paxton raised his notebook, gesturing to the meadow. "You know the young man down there?"

"I do. Or—" She gave a slight shake of her head. "I mean I did. Every four years the town's council finances an applicant with a full scholarship to Conifer College. Vyvan Wood is—*was* the most recent scholarship winner." Her lip quivered. "This was only his second semester."

Paxton twiddled his pen. "Ms. Black—"

"Celeste, please." She bestowed a watery smile.

"Can you tell us if this young man had any enemies? Anybody who'd want to hurt him?"

Celeste shook her head. "No, not that I know of. He was a quiet, reserved young man. Always very polite. He was studying business and philosophy."

"Any family?" Lance asked.

Celeste shook her head again. "His parents died in a car accident when he was a kid. He was raised by his grandmother but she died last year. He didn't have anyone left, so we—the council board, I mean—took him under our wing."

"Why would someone have wanted to hurt him then?" I looked out over the field. The grass hid the majority of the college student from view. Was this a ritualistic killing or a show? Something about the scene indicated it was the former, but whatever it was eluded me.

Celeste bit her lip. "Forgive me, I know I should never have seen it, but did I see runes etched into the ground around the—the body?"

Runes. Interesting that she'd identify them that way. I turned back around to see Paxton nodding. "You didn't recognize them, did you?"

She shook her head, but she paused first, standing straighter and her expression closing off.

Paxton and I glanced at one another.

Lance cleared his throat. "Thank you for your help, Ms. Black, but I think we've taken up enough of your time. Let me walk you to your car."

Celeste appeared taken aback, but she nodded. "Of course. It was a pleasure to meet you, Agent Holt, Dr. Grace."

Paxton handed me a card and I wrote my number on the back before handing it to her. "If you think of anything else, please don't hesitate to reach out."

The Sheriff and Celeste walked towards her gray Audi.

I turned back again to the field, watching the officers continue to document the area, nowhere near the body.

Movement at the forest line behind the body caught my eye. I squinted.

A figure stood in the shadow of the trees.

14

Holt

Sheriff Lance, much to my irritation, told us he and his team would undertake Vyvan Wood's background check, directing us to investigate the lilies and symbols around the body. There was something in the way he gave us instructions that rubbed me the wrong way. But I swallowed my annoyance as we discussed our course of action. According to Willow, there was only one floral shop in town, so that was the best place to start asking about the lilies. We all were to meet back up at the Conifer precinct later that afternoon to compare notes.

Willow and I were quiet as we drove the long, winding road back into town.

The sky was starting to turn gray again, a few sunbeams forcing through the cracks in the vapor. I inhaled, catching both the familiar smell of the car and the faint scent of Willow's shampoo. I glanced at her and saw she was rereading the case file and typing away on her phone, likely adding notes.

Vyvan Wood was yet another victim of the organ trafficking ring. Something in my gut made me one hundred percent certain which made it hard not to let it cloud my judgment.

However, convinced as I was that all the staging—the flowers, the runes—was just a ruse, I couldn't help but wonder about what Willow had pointed out: what *was* the point of all the theatrics?

We had closed the trafficking operation down and, barring the bewildering lack of bodies, the thing that had bothered me most was the traffickers' total cooperation after we arrested them. As if they had known they'd get caught all along. I gripped the steering wheel as the winding road straightened out. The trees thinned out and we passed more cars. Downtown Conifer was up ahead.

I must have missed something, after all. But what?

"That poor steering wheel will suffocate under that grip if you don't loosen up."

I relaxed my vice-like grip on at the sound of Willow's voice. "No kidding. I guess I should charge myself."

I glanced over at her, admiring how her body swayed with the car's motion.

Her face deadpan, Willow said, "Might be fun to see you in handcuffs."

I stared at her, my seatbelt suddenly too tight. She started laughing.

"I *have* seen you in handcuffs," I said, "and it about broke my heart."

Willow scrunched her face, her expression full of distaste. "Thanks for the dose of cold water."

I grabbed her hand over the center console. "Working, we're supposed to be working."

"I know." She squeezed my fingers. A soft smile spread across her lips. "But you looked so tense. I wanted to break the ice."

I smiled back before turning my attention back to the road. The serious nature of the case came over both of us and the teasing atmosphere hardened.

Willow shook her head. "What is it with stealing either people or body parts?"

I huffed, wondering the same thing. In our last assigned case, we had uncovered a child trafficking ring. In the case before that, a psycho trying to reassemble a person I had long put to rest. Ultimately, when it came to brass tacks, most crimes were theft. Murder stole life. Rape stole autonomy. Trafficking *was* stealing, regardless of the cargo. Criminals were all thieves of some kind.

"Do you really think these are the same organ traffickers from the Rendezvous case?" Willow asked.

"I wouldn't bet the outcome of the case on it, but from what I've seen, yes. Remember the crime scene photos of Baily's body? Even with that gaping hole in his chest, he wasn't laying in a pool of blood." I tightened my jaw before I could continue. "Neither was the vic here. It appears to me that neither had their hearts exhumed where their bodies were found. Additionally, just from the naked eye, it's clear that the crude incision marks are identical."

"What does that indicate, though?" Willow asked. "Both had their hearts taken away by someone less than competent to do so."

"Typically I would agree with you, but it's the sameness that caught my eye. Around the holes in both Baily and Vyvan Woods' chests were four deeper, more jagged incisions. Then, as if sawed away, the flesh and the rib bones were removed. I would expect similar surgical markings in a legal procedure. But in an illegal one? That doesn't make sense."

Willow chewed her lip.

"You disagree?"

"Not exactly." She shifted in her seat to face me, even though I kept my gaze trained on the road. "I know you're set on this being an off shoot of the ring, and maybe you're right. What you described is suspicious. But why would traffickers go through all the trouble to set up something so ritualistic, down to the symbolism?"

That's why it didn't make sense.

"Why lilies?" I asked aloud.

"Lilies are often associated with purity and innocence," Willow said.

I gave a slow nod.

"I just wanna know where the lilies came from," Willow said. "They aren't native to Washington, so if they aren't from the florist shop, I'm stumped."

I grunted. "Did you see the way Celeste became a brick wall when I asked if she recognized the markings around the body?"

Willow eyes widened as she nodded. "Or that she identified the markings around the body as 'runes'? Most people would call them markings or symbols unless they had an inkling of what they were."

Willow nodded again. "Yes, I noted that as well."

I flipped the turn signal on, waiting for a gray Audi coming the opposite way to make the same turn onto the main street of downtown Conifer.

"Glad we're on the same page."

Fifteen minutes later, after we had parked, we walked into *Huckleberry's Finest* florist shop. The small establishment was housed in a room made of all right angles, from the walls to the shelves, to the windows. The only curves to the place were from the flowers and greenery covering every surface.

I didn't recognize most of the plants, but Willow walked around, smiling at the flowers and touching the ends of the plants hanging from the ceiling. Standing on the tips of her toes, she brought her face to a pink flower that spilled over the edge of its pot. A rare streak of sun caught Willow, capturing her silhouette to perfection.

An image of her watering plants in nothing but one of my button-up work shirts crossed my mind.

"Can I help you?" A brusque voice asked.

I turned to see a man dressed all in loose, multicolored clothing leaning over the counter. His hands and arms were rough and dry, indicating he worked hard with them. Dark round glasses were perched on his small nose. A nametag with the name *Huck* was pinned to his neon pink bucket hat.

I pulled out my badge. "Agent Holt, FBI. We have some questions regarding a recent purchase of flowers. Are you the owner?"

He glanced at Willow, who had walked over to stand beside me, before turning his watery gaze back to me.

"Yes, I am. The name's Huckleberry, but Huck will do." His voice was now tinged with curiosity.

I pulled out my notebook and pen. "We're looking for someone who recently bought lilies."

Huck's bright red eyebrows rose up. "Lilies?"

"That's right. Anyone purchase a couple dozen lilies from you? Within the last thirty-six hours."

"I doubt it," Huck said, scoffing. "I don't sell lilies."

"Really? How come?"

"They cost a fortune to import since they aren't a local flower. And on top of that, they stink to high heaven."

Willow hid a smile at this frank statement. "Is there any other place in town that might sell lilies?"

Huck shook his head. "Nope. The only place to buy flowers worth beans in this town is here. And I don't sell lilies. Now is there something else I can help you with?"

"Yes," Willow said, her already kind tone taking on an even warmer cadence. "I'm sure you know all the local flora and fauna. On our way here we saw some lovely landscaping. Does everyone get their flowers from you?"

Huck beamed at this. "There are some lovely estates in the area. Many of them get the majority of their garden treasures from me, but if a customer wants something special they have to import it themselves."

Willow hummed. "Do you know if anybody has ever ordered any nonlocal flora?"

Huck tapped his chin, his movements exaggerated though not mocking. "I know that ol' Madame Morgana loved lilies. I think she had some in her greenhouse on her estate."

"As in Morgana Ravenwood?" I asked.

Huck tapped the side of his nose. "The very one. She had all kinds of imported flowers. Lilies, Orange Mock, Dahlias—"

"That's great." I glanced at Willow to make sure she didn't have any further questions. She gave me a covert shake of her head. "Huck, this was really helpful, thank you."

"Sure, sure." Huck swept his hand out in front of him. "Now were you gonna buy something?"

"Actually, yes." I pointed to the hanging plant that Willow had been admiring a few moments before. "Ring me up that one."

15

Willow

I hummed with contentment as Paxton crossed the street to place my new plant baby in the car.

"You didn't have to do that, you know," I said when he returned.

He gave me a lopsided grin. "Do what?"

"Buy something to appease that old wart."

"I merely observed you enjoying those flowers and thought you'd like to have them."

I smiled at him, my heart swelling.

Paxton gave me a small wink before looking at his phone. "We still have a little while before we report back to Lance. Coffee?"

"You read my mind."

I led the way up the street to Olympia Coffee Roasters, pointing out different shops and relaying small anecdotes from when I lived in the area. I had met clients and students alike over the years, each with a story similar to my own. Thinking about their stories brought Vyvan

Woods to mind, and a fresh wave of sadness threatened to leak from my eyes. I hadn't known him, but from Celeste's description, he seemed like a decent kid. It was a waste and a shame that his life was cut so short.

The Apothecary's dark windows still drew my eyes from across the street as we approached the coffee shop. I wondered how Cynthia was doing in the wake of Morgana's passing. I made a mental note to check in with Malcolm.

We walked up to the coffee shop, passing the outside table and chairs, now all opened up as if intent on tempting the sun to stay out. A few patrons sat chatting as Paxton held the café door open for me and another couple who had walked in behind us. I caught sight of a gray vehicle parked up the street outside the Apothecary before Paxton stepped inside and the door swung shut behind him, restricting my view of the car. The smell of the blueberry muffins brought my attention to the pastry display cabinet.

I admired the array of baked goods while we waited in line. When it came our turn, I ordered a lavender latte and Paxton a black coffee before we sat in my favorite booth at the back corner. I noted most tables were empty today, though that was unsurprising in the middle of a weekday.

As I put my coat on the chair beside me, Paxton's phone rang in his pocket. He pulled it out, read the caller ID, mouthed, "It's Del," and answered.

"'Sup kid, hold on a second. Need to step outside."

He nodded to me and headed out. I caught a barista's attention and told her we would be right back before following Paxton outside. A landline started ringing as the door closed behind me.

Paxton was sitting at one of the tables, eyes partially squinted in the early afternoon light. He pulled the phone away from his head when he saw me. "Ah, here she is." He turned the speakerphone on.

"Hi, Del," I said, sitting across the table from him.

"Ah, lovely," she replied. "Hey Ax, Willow. Do you guys have a minute?"

"Sure do," Paxton said, "but only a minute."

"I'll be brief then. Willow, remember ages ago one of your students was an old friend of mine? Caroline?"

I smiled at the phone as I leaned back in my metal seat, crossing one leg over the other. "Sure do. She reached out to you?"

"Correct! Wanna guess what about?"

Caroline had followed through. "She called to tell you about a potential Alaska gig?"

"Right again! The camp needs volunteers. Doesn't pay anything, but free room and board."

"What kind of volunteer work?" Paxton asked.

"They have a barn and a big kitchen. She told me general maintenance. Not sure on specifics."

"So, whatcha thinking?" I asked her, glancing up at Paxton. He was tapping the edge of the table with his thumb.

"I... I dunno." Del admitted. "If I accepted, they'd want me to come up as soon as I can and I'd stay through the summer, so about six months total. Never been a big connoisseur of the outdoors, but it's *Alaska*. Talk about the opportunity of a lifetime—"

The café door opened and Suza walked out and put our drinks and some napkins on the table. She and I exchanged a smile of recognition before she gave a pronounced nod to the drinks and disappeared back inside.

"So..." Del said. "Any thoughts?"

"It sounds like an amazing opportunity, Del," I said as I pulled my drink towards me. "I think you should do the research, and if you feel like it's a safe and good thing, then get outta here."

"That's kind of what I was thinking you'd say."

"Do you think this opportunity will stick?" I asked.

She paused before replying. "Yes, I do. Also, Caroline mentioned that you put in a word for me. Thanks for having my back."

"Of course."

She let the silence lapse again, as if waiting for one of us to say more. "What about you, Ax?"

Paxton leaned back in his seat, putting the phone on the table. He picked up his coffee but didn't drink it.

"Ax?"

"I think, if it's what you want to do, you should do it." He paused. "I think, as much as I'm glad you're asking for opinions, that you already know what the best thing for you to do is. So go for it, kid. You have mine and Willow's full support."

I took Paxton's hand and squeezed it. "As always."

"In fairness though, there is an element of necessity as my mom's house is about to close. Did I tell you about that? I got a buyer and signed the papers."

Paxton and I both congratulated her.

"Thanks. I think..." She took a deep breath. "I think I'll tell those Alaskan peeps I'll take the job. Maybe I should rent out my house while I'm gone? Sinsae always said I could crash at her place, so maybe I'll take her up on that offer. Maybe Solomon and Sinsae will help me move my stuff into storage? Geez, I have a million things to do now."

We all chuckled, and Paxton's eyes flooded with a little sadness mixed heavily with pride. "Kid, this is great news. I'm proud of you."

"It's all kinda sudden if you ask me. But thanks. I'll keep you guys in the loop."

Paxton and I both stated our thanks. I uncrossed my legs and bumped the table, causing coffee to slosh down the side of my cup. I picked up a few napkins from the pile and started wiping the coffee drops on the table.

"So are y'all on a new case?" Del asked.

"Yep, we were handed a new one this morning," I said.

I picked up the napkins and the pile splayed out. I spotted something on the bottom napkin. I moved to look at it.

"Gotcha. I won't ask anymore—" Del grew silent. I stopped my movement and Paxton and I looked at each other. Before I could ask her if everything was okay, her voice broke the silence again. "Look on the bottom napkin by Willow's drink."

Paxton and I exchanged another look, and I pulled the bottom napkin from the pile.

I inhaled, about to ask how she knew to look when she spoke again. "I gotta go. Thanks guys, love you!"

Then she disconnected the call.

Paxton put his phone back in his pocket as I handed him the napkin. An orange sticky note was stuck to it.

> *Please be so kind as to meet me at the amphitheater on the Lawn. I have something that might be pertinent to the case.*
>
> *~Celeste*

16

Willow

PAXTON AND I WALKED TO THE LAWN, ONLY ABOUT A BLOCK from the coffee shop. The collection of man-made park areas was carved out of a hillside, about two stories lower than the rest of the town.

"Love that girl to death," I said as we started walking down the stairs. "But that niece of yours—"

"Has an uncanny way of knowing things?" Paxton finished for me.

"Exactly. One of these days I'm going to pin that girl down and get an answer out of her for always knowing things she shouldn't."

We reached the bottom of the steps. Straight ahead of us, a group of highschoolers kicked a ball around a maintained soccer field, with fresh white lines and framed goal nets.

As we got to the landing and turned right, we passed a play park with half a dozen children running amok. Several adults gathered close by near the picnic tables and benches. They faced the park though some hovered over their phones or tablets while others chatted amongst themselves.

The small amphitheater appeared past the picnic benches, a stone backdrop behind two rows of five multicolored wooden benches. Moss grew between the cracks of the wood slats and patches of lichen dotted the metal frames.

A woman sat in the second to last row on the right. A black scarf covered her head, hiding the color of her hair from the back. A patch of porcelain skin peeked out between the scarf and collar of her rain jacket. Our footsteps echoed against the cobblestone walkway and the woman turned around and raised her rhinestone-studded cat-eyed sunglasses.

"You got my note," Celeste said, standing as we approached and gesturing to the bench in front of her.

I stepped down the row ahead of Paxton and sat, raising one leg onto the seat and putting my right arm over the back of the bench so I could better face Celeste. Paxton remained standing, resting his tail bone against the back of the bench of the row ahead of us and pulling out his notebook.

"How did you get that note to us?" He asked her. "Never saw you enter the shop."

"I'm friends with the baristas. When I saw you had gone in—"

"You were watching us?"

"I was going to call the station," Celeste ever so slightly bristled, "To see if I could find you, but I happened to be in the area and noticed you two had walked into Roasters." Celeste pulled her jacket tighter around her frame. "I called the shop, gave the barista on duty instructions to get you a note, and promised her a generous tip the next time I came in."

Paxton raised his eyebrow. "And they just do stuff like that for you?"

Celeste shrugged, though the corner of her mouth lifted. "I'm a reliable sort."

So this wasn't the first time that she bribed someone into doing something for her. Wondering what that meant for our conversation now, I laid my left hand on my thigh.

"You couldn't have just come in to talk to us?" I asked.

She shook her head. "Too risky. You never know who might be listening. Besides," a lofty grin grew on her red mouth, "it got your attention."

"You definitely have our attention," Paxton said. "You have something to tell us you don't want your boyfriend to hear?"

"Boyfriend?" Celeste rolled her eyes, but her face flushed. "As if Sheriff Lance would be so lucky."

I had to bite back a snort. No one had said anything about Sheriff Lance. Seemed like Paxton's observation about them was correct.

"Look at me, do I look like the sort a law enforcement type would date?"

"You'd be surprised what law enforcement types are in to," Paxton said.

"This is *not* why I asked you to meet me here." Celeste shook her head, and Paxton gave me a covert wink. "Maybe this wasn't a good idea," she muttered under her breath.

"Hey, you asked us here, remember?" Paxton crossed his arms. "If you know something that could assist in our investigation, tell us. Please."

Celeste sucked in a breath and placed her hands on her knees. "I know I said otherwise, but... I recognized the runes around the body."

Celeste leaned forward. "I'll admit I wasn't entirely honest, but it wasn't exactly a lie either. I wasn't sure if I *did* recognize them at first. But none of this will make sense unless I start from the beginning."

Paxton clicked his pen and opened his notebook to a new page. "Please do."

"Have either of you met Morgana Ravenwood?"

"Yes," I said. "Once."

Celeste gave me a single nod. "Then you may know Morgana Ravenwood was the beating heart of Conifer. She made this place a home for hundreds of people. She's helped lower the number of homeless people on the streets, start businesses, fund scholarships, and started so many community programs. She even helped refurbish Conifer College."

A sad smile formed on Celeste's red lips. "She was also my mentor. In addition to being a generous paragon of society, she was warm, kind, and encouraging. You couldn't have met a lovelier woman. She was the maternal figure I never really had in my life."

This matched with my limited knowledge of the woman. I couldn't count the number of events she hosted at the college. She was always up giving speeches, presiding over charity events, and giving to the community.

"I'm sure you saw the news that she passed away a few weeks ago?" Celeste asked, glancing between the two of us.

"I was quite surprised by that," I said. "I met a friend in the Apothecary the day before she died, and we happened upon Morgana. She seemed in perfect health to me."

"It was a shock to all who knew her." Celeste closed her eyes, as if envisioning the scene. "A freak accident. She slipped on some water and hit her head on the edge of the mantle in her office."

Paxton began tapping his pen against the side of his leg. I glanced at him and he gave me a brief look, his jaw tight.

Celeste didn't seem to notice. She continued. "Two days before she died, Morgana called me to her home. She was distracted and as much as she tried to hide it, I could tell she was anxious. When I asked her what was wrong, she assured me everything was fine. I didn't believe her but I was hesitant to push too much. She gave me this."

Celeste pulled out a black, leatherbound notebook. She handed it to me and I took it, the journal denser than I'd anticipated. A metal hinge clasped it shut. I unlatched it and it fell open in my palms. A whiff of old paper blew out of the yellow, crinkled pages. The script inside appeared similar to Nordic runes. Paxton looked over my shoulder at the book. "Ms. Black, how is this relevant?"

Celeste leaned forward and closed the book in my hands, pointing to a symbol on the front cover. It was the same as the third symbol in the repeating pattern around the body.

I looked into the other woman's eyes, but they were still on the book. "Why didn't you bring this to the police after Morgana was found dead?"

Paxton straightened. "Or, more importantly, when you suspected the runes around the dead boy's body to be the same?"

"I'm here now, aren't I?" Celeste leaned back, hugging herself. "If Morgana had died by foul play, then there might have been something to it. But investigators proved her death to be an accident."

"Do you believe that?" Paxton asked.

"I do," Celeste said. "She didn't have enemies. She was alone in the house at the time of her death. That notebook is the only thing that made me wonder if there was something else going on."

I opened the pages again, tracing over the script with my index finger. "Can you read this? Do you know what language it's written in?"

She shook her head. "No, unfortunately. Otherwise, I would have already translated it and maybe had more information to give you. But I know it's ancient." A small smile passed over her lips. "Morgana took to tinkering with archaic languages and alphabets. One of her many hobbies. Unfortunately, I have reason to believe the books she had in her library that might have helped with this have recently been removed."

Paxton looked up from his notes, eyes narrowed. "How do you know?"

"Last time I saw her, I noticed that some of the books on her shelf were missing. I haven't a clue where they might have gone and the only person that I could ask, I'm, uh, hesitant to do so."

"Who would that be?" I asked.

"Morgana's granddaughter, Selena."

"Why are you hesitant?"

Celeste puckered her lips again. "Selena's going through a lot right now. She's taken the death of her grandmother very hard. I don't want to burden her with this. But also, I don't know why Morgana gave me the notebook and not her." She tapped her toes on the ground. "I'm worried that there's more than meets the eye."

"I don't know how much good us having this notebook will do, then," I said. "Unless you know of someone who can translate it for us?"

"I do." To my surprise, Celeste huffed. "There's a gentleman in town who probably could."

Paxton grunted. "Sounds like there's a story there as to why you haven't already gone to him."

"Let's just say that Dr. Abernathy and I don't see eye to eye on most things." Celeste's nostrils flared for a second. "He's an ass, but he knows his stuff."

"I take it there's no one else who might be able to translate it for us?" I asked.

Celeste shook her head slowly. "Not anymore. Morgana used to have a bookkeeper, but I haven't seen him around in a while."

That *definitely* wasn't related to anything. I glanced at Paxton again and saw he had made note of what Celeste had said too. More questions were starting to dangle around us.

Pressing my hand to my face, I asked, "Who was that person?"

"Never knew his name. Morgana always referred to him as—" she stopped, as if preventing herself from misstepping. "Kay. But to my knowledge Dr. Abernathy's it. If you take that notebook to him and tell him that it used to belong to Morgana, he'll help you." Celeste told us his address, and Paxton wrote it down. "Best to keep my name out of it though, if you can."

I shut and re-clasped the notebook, dust flying out of its creases. "We'll see what we can do."

"One more question, Celeste." Paxton tapped his notebook with his pen. "Any stock in the rumor of there being a coven of witches in the area?"

A gust of wind caught our hair. Paxton clutched his notebook to his chest to prevent the pages from flapping. I smoothed my hair out of my face and grabbed it at the base of my neck.

"A coven of witches?" Celeste laughed, buttoning the top button of her black raincoat. "Absolutely not. There're some odd people in the area, I grant you, and yes, Conifer has that new Apothecary store now, but there is no *coven*. We simply like to embrace the odd, allow people the freedom to practice what they will, and honor the history of the place."

She stood and Paxton and I followed suit. She slid her glasses on her face before saying "Believe me, in a town this small, I would know if there were witches."

17

Celeste

CELESTE WATCHED DR. GRACE AND AGENT HOLT RETREAT UP the stairs back into town. Halfway up, Dr. Grace tucked the journal into her coat. Agent Holt looked back and said something, his brows furrowed. Dr. Grace shrugged in response. She then passed him, turning her head to him and speaking. Her face softened and she smiled at him. Agent Holt nodded, warmth growing on his face as placed his hand on her lower back. Then the two were out of Celeste's line of sight.

She could tell they didn't trust her. She couldn't blame them. What a fool she must have looked like earlier, rushing in on a crime scene as if she were a security guard for the Estate. She had forgotten herself and whom she was dealing with.

The look Terran had given her when he guided her back up to the vehicles. A mix of smugness and sympathy so prevalent she almost couldn't stand it. Celeste's cheeks warmed at the memory.

Cheeky bastard.

Still, it was vital that the doctor and FBI agent be given the right information. The pertinent information. It was more than her own secrets she had to protect, after all.

A rustling in the bushes caught Celeste's eye. She turned to the edge of the amphitheater and scanned the bushes and trees lining the area. A prickling sensation formed on the back of her neck, but after a few more seconds of scanning, the feeling of being watched dissipated. Still, she took it as a sign to leave.

Celeste walked past the stairs, the playground, the soccer field. Past all the children, so focused on playing. So pure in their fun. So very innocent.

Poor Vyvan.

Tears formed in her eyes. Though she hadn't known him well nor very long, she had liked him. He had been polite and grateful for the opportunity the council had given him. But his death complicated things. Would it be worth the cost of everyone's rising panic?

The pavement gave way to a desire path in the grass. Celeste glanced behind her, but no one paid her any mind. Most people didn't realize just how big the Ravenwood Estate really was. No one would notice a little woman heading for the tree line that marked the beginning of the private estate.

She made her way down the soft decline into the woods. In the safety and privacy of the trees, her shoulders relaxed. The forest hummed around her in a song of rustling, snapping, and scurrying.

Breathe, Celeste. Morgana's voice echoed in her head. *Breathe. Feel the energy around you and be at peace.*

With the mess you left me in? Not likely.

The last time she ever saw Morgana, a week before the older woman had died, had been playing on repeat in her mind. The loop started again as she walked through the intermittent underbrush.

Morgana was pacing in her study when Celeste opened the door, chilled and damp from the downpour she'd had to rush through.

Morgana beckoned her in, continuing her pacing. Celeste closed the door behind her, walked to the loveseat, and sat.

Morgana didn't say anything. Celeste waited, the crackling fire warming her to her bones. She glanced around the room to be sure nothing was amiss. It wasn't. Everything was as tidy and organized as it had always been. The pitcher of water was still on the side table. The bearskin rug was still intact. The large, cherry wood desk was cleared of everything, save the lamp, feathered pen, and inkwell.

Then her gaze drifted to the bookshelf behind the desk. Some books were missing from the highest shelf. But she couldn't tell which ones.

Morgana stopped pacing, seeming to notice that Celeste was present. "Celeste, forgive me. I'm glad you've come."

She walked over and sat down on the open cushion, taking Celeste's hands between her smooth, soft, ice-cold palms.

"What's ailing you?" Celeste asked, concern growing at Morgana's distracted countenance.

But Morgana shook her head. "Nothing, my dear. Nothing. I know that this is unusual, but I promise nothing is amiss." Her voice was normal, even soothing.

Celeste's shoulders relaxed, her body easing. Morgana then splayed her hands out so that she could trace a finger over Celeste's palm and wrist. Something caught at Celeste's mind, but she lost it before she could place what it was.

Refocusing on the conversation, Celeste asked, "And the coven?"

"As it ought to be."

Celeste took in a deep, calming breath. "I am glad to hear it."

"My dear." Morgana rubbed her thumbs over Celeste's knuckles. "I have done everything I can for the best of others. You believe me when I say that, don't you?"

"Of course! It has always been so. I've seen it with my own eyes to be true."

Morgana dipped her head, her silver hair falling over her shoulders. "I have not always been perfect, but I've done everything with the best of intentions for all." She saw Celeste's face and chuckled. "Don't be so troubled, child. It is no matter. The ramblings of an old woman."

She let go of Celeste's hands and pulled a black leatherbound book out from the pocket of her flowing robes. "I have a task for you."

Celeste leaned forward. "Of course, my lady. Anything."

Morgana placed the book into Celeste's lap. "I need you to keep this safe."

"What is it?"

"A record," Morgana said. "Call it a ledger, diary, journal, whatever you fancy. I need you to look after it for me."

"Of course I will, but—" Celeste looked down at the notebook, eyes tracing the unfamiliar rune on the front cover. "Why me? Why not the Keeper of Knowledge?"

"This is a more personal affair than I wish Kay to be privy to."

Celeste looked back up at her mistress. "What about Selena?"

"I don't carry all my eggs in one basket, dear. You know this."

Celeste looked into Morgana's eyes, searching for a deeper explanation, but she didn't elaborate.

"Thank you, my dear." Morgana placed her hand on Celeste's cheek. "You're giving me peace of mind."

How much Celeste regretted never learning how to read the old runes. But neither she nor Selena had made it that far in their training. Now they never would.

Celeste stumbled over a rock, but she remained upright. Heart pounding, she looked up to see the back of a giant stone structure. Morgana's grave.

The giant stone lion looked down from his perch. He stood tall above the ground, chest puffed out and frozen mane blew with a silent breeze. His mouth turned down in mourning.

Celeste rounded the monument to read the inscription on the ledger stone covering Morgana's remains, running her fingers over the engraving. *A Beating Heart Proves There is More to Life Than Mere Blood*

Morgana's heart had been beating, but something had been wrong. Celeste hadn't realized until much later, after going over and over her last encounter in her mind. When Morgana had taken her hand, Celeste had felt the other woman's pulse, its rhythm jagged and off-beat.

Celeste thumped her fist against the grave. Damn it all. She was on her own in this. She hoped to the earth and stars that Dr. Grace and Agent Holt could do something. Selena had been a shell of herself since Morgana had died.

As Celeste looked around the clearing, a memory from when she and Selena were teenagers crossed her mind.

"Girls!" Morgana's voice called through the dusk, her voice carrying far further than it should have. "Come. The first here will get a glimpse into the Forbidden Book."

The Forbidden Book. That which only a chosen few ever got to read, whom even fewer could understand. The secrets of their very world were written in those pages.

The two of them looked at each other, dropped their foraging baskets, and started running to the house. Despite Selena's longer legs, Celeste was faster. She weaved through the trees and dashed across the clearing, remembering to dodge the rabbit holes.

Just as she was closing in on the house, a crack and a scream rent the air. Celeste skirted to a stop, looking around. Selena was laying sprawled on the ground, her foot bent sideways, toes pointing in a position they never would naturally.

Celeste looked to the house, seeing Morgana's figure outlined by the inside lights. standing there. She was so close. She could run and reach Morgana, claiming ignorance to Selena's plight. But she heard her whimpering behind her and knew she couldn't do it.

She ran back to Selena.

"What are you doing?" Selena's voice cracked as Celeste knelt beside her. "You won, damn it. Do you have to rub it in?"

"No. It doesn't count if both of us don't come back." Celeste reached a hand out to her friend. "We'll tie."

Selena's tearstained face lifted. She allowed Celeste to hook her arms under hers and heave her up. Together, the two of them made it back to the house.

Morgana stood watching them as they approached the back porch door. She waved her hand and Selena stood a little straighter, though she still winced when she put pressure on her foot.

"Tied." Morgana looked between the girls. "But Celeste would have won if she hadn't decided to go back." She held her hand out to Celeste and beckoned her forward.

Celeste took a hesitant step forward, looking back at Selena. Selena's face was brick-red, fresh tears leaking down her face. Celeste allowed Morgana to lead her away.

Celeste blinked the memory away. It had been a long time ago. Reminiscing wouldn't help with anything now. She wished she could ask the Keeper of Knowledge for help, but he'd vanished without a trace a week or so after Morgana had died. Yet another bad omen.

She had to place her hope in the detectives being discrete. No point in worrying the coven or the townsfolk if she didn't have to. She relaxed her fist and placed her hand flat on the cool gravestone, trying to connect to the energy beneath. What had Morgana written in that ledger?

The ledger. *Let that old fool prove his usefulness one last time.*

The ledger had to be the key to everything.

18

Holt

"You get the impression that Celeste Black was hiding something?" Willow asked as we started walking back towards the stairs.

I glanced over my shoulder at Celeste who was still standing in the amphitheater. "One hundred percent."

"Did you notice the way she talked about Selena?" Willow asked. "Her voice hitched when she mentioned her."

"I did notice that," I said as we started climbing the stairs. "Perhaps Morgana favored her over her own granddaughter?"

"Maybe." Willow stopped on the stairs and looked down at the notebook she was still holding. She tucked it into her coat pocket. "It's just odd."

"Think she's connected to the coven idea somehow?" I asked.

Willow looked at me. "It's possible. She certainly is well

connected—" she stopped, catching the frown on my face. "What? You still think that angle is bogus?"

I raised my hands. "Just waiting to be convinced."

"Well, I think it's plausible."

"The doctor has spoken."

She shook her head at me, but a smile was growing on her face.

I grinned back, touching her lowering back. We resumed walking.

As we rounded the corner back to the main street, Willow's phone rang. We stepped to the side as she pulled it out but frowned as she read the caller ID. She glanced at me before answering.

"Hello, this is Dr. Grace." She paused and her face brightened. "Brutus!"

I frowned and furrowed my brows in a question at her. She mouthed *Kincaid's guard* to me. I furrowed my brows further until I remembered her telling me about the middle-aged guard that she always chatted with in and out of interviewing Kincaid. He was the one with the sick daughter. I didn't recollect that he had ever called her before.

"Hi, what's up? Is everything okay?" She said into the phone. Her own brows were furrowed as she listened "Is it Annie? Is she alright?" Her shoulders relaxed. "Oh, good. Well, then, why'd you—" Her eyes widened.

She stood there listening and I started tapping my leg.

"Thanks, Brutus. I appreciate you letting me know. Yes, alright. Talk soon." She pulled the phone from her face and tapped the screen.

"What was that about?"

Willow slipped the phone back into her pocket, biting her lower lip. "Kincaid requested Brutus call with a message."

I stared at her. "Why did Brutus listen to that? Not go through the proper channels?"

"He told me he reported it to McCannon right away but that McCannon told him to go ahead and call me."

Alarm bells started going off in my mind. "Well, what did Kincaid have to say?"

Willow rubbed the side of her mouth. "He said 'gates often lead to more questions than answers.'"

"That's it?"

"I know." She bit her lower lip again. "Why would Kincaid go to the trouble?"

After giving her a moment to ponder, I reached over and touched her shoulder. "We should get rolling."

Murphy met us at the front door of the precinct and led the way into the small station. The whole building smelled of old food, bad coffee, and printer ink. It was a small office, with only a handful of desks set at right angles to each other in a large open room. Lance's desk was in the corner, walled off by portable cloth wall separators. Murphy led us past the empty desk and into the break room, which, based on the number of dry erase and cork boards hung on the wall, led me to believe it was also their conference room.

Lance greeted us as we entered and flicked on the light. Willow sat in one of the metal chairs, crossing one leg over the other and folding her hands together. Murphy crossed the room to the little dorm fridge and turned on the coffee pot sitting on top.

A couple other officers filed in and took their seats, some pulling notebooks out. I stayed standing, walking a few paces into the room before turning back to see Lance sitting on the edge of a table pushed against the wall.

He looked contemplative, his eyes unfocused as I moved to stand beside Willow. I brushed her shoulder and she gave me a brief smile before we both turned to the sheriff. The gurgling noises of the coffee pot filled the short silence as everyone settled.

"This is Special Agent Holt and Dr. Willow Grace," Lance said to the room, gesturing towards us. "I'm sure you saw them at the crime scene this morning. They've been assigned to help us solve the Ravenwood case. Please do everything you can to assist and help them feel welcome."

Murmured acknowledgments drifted our way as I nodded and Willow raised a hand in greeting.

"Let's have an update on what we've discovered so far." Lance picked up a dry erase marker and pointed at one of the officers, a spotty young man with bright red hair. "Sainz, talk to me."

Sainz had been one of the officers putting flags around the crime scene when we'd arrived. He sat up straighter in his chair and began.

"Vic's name is Vyvan Woods, aged nineteen, orphaned after his folks died in a car crash when he was eight. He hopped around foster homes until he was eighteen when he got accepted to Conifer College.

"Murphy and I went to the vic's place of residence and were able to chat with both of his roommates." Sainz inhaled a breath through his nose and shook his head. "Honestly sir, this kid was kinda boring, all things considered. He went to the university as a fulltime student and worked at the local pizza joint as a delivery driver. He had two roommates, also college students, whom Vyvan was on decent terms with."

Lance wrote the information in bullet points on the board. "Both roommates had alibis?"

"Yes sir. One was in a lab class from eight am to eleven am and the other was in the library, studying with some classmates from seven-thirty am to noon when he then headed to his next class.

"Both said Vyvan was a night owl, with his classes in the afternoon and his shift hours in the evening, so they rarely saw him during the week." Sainz winced. "Today was no exception."

"They didn't check to see if he was still in the house before they left?" Lance asked.

Sainz shook his head. "No, his door's usually closed in the mornings, so they both assumed he was asleep."

"What about his car?" I asked.

"He and his roommates shared a car," Sainz said. "So they had it this morning."

Murphy spoke up in the moment of silence. "His roommates did say that he had a bit of fascination with the occult."

"What do you mean?" Lance asked.

Murphy glanced at Sainz before continuing. "He liked to watch true crime documentaries and listen to podcasts about the occult and macabre. Occasionally burned incense too."

"Dude." Sainz rolled his eyes, tone indicating they'd already discussed this. "Burning incense is a totally common occurrence. Churches have been doing it for centuries."

Murphy raised his hands in surrender. "I hate incense so forgive me for thinking it's weird, man."

"Maybe you're just biased."

"And maybe you're—"

"Guys!" Lance cut in. "Let's get back to the topic at hand, please."

"That's it, boss," Sainz said. "He was a hard-working kid with a *mild*"—he glanced at Murphy—"interest in the occult."

"And honestly," Willow said, "what with the rise in popularity of consuming true crime, it isn't all that strange to be interested in the occult too."

"Maybe this occult interest was purely coincidental." Lance rubbed his finger and thumb out along his mustache. "But say it wasn't. Maybe there's something there." He pointed to us. "Tell me what you guys got."

Willow described our investigation into the lilies and receiving the note from Celeste. Lance's jaw tightened at the mention of the woman but didn't interrupt as I took over the narrative, briefing him on our encounter with her. Willow took out the leatherbound notebook when I was done, splaying it out in her palms and opening the pages. Lance walked over to inspect the notebook more closely.

"It's looks to be nothing but a ledger, really." Willow pointed to symbols written in the margins around lines of numbers. "Barring the fact that everything else is written in old runes. And speaking of old runes"—Willow closed the book and pointed to the symbol etched into the front cover—"Look at this one."

The sheriff narrowed his gaze at it before pulling out his phone. He swiped for a few minutes and pulled up a picture from the crime scene. He compared the image to the notebook's front cover. On the screen was a zoomed in picture of the three glyphs we had seen carved into the dirt.

"The very same."

Willow nodded.

Lance straightened and repocketed his phone. "And you said this book belonged to Morgana Ravenwood?"

"Yes."

"Who is the same person to whom the field belongs, who is the only known person in the area who grows the kind of lilies found at the crime scene, *and* who apparently can write in the same foreign language as the symbols around the body?"

"Yep." Willow popped the 'p'.

"We need to get those symbols translated." Lance walked over to the board and started writing notes. "And there's someone in town who might be able to do just that."

Lance dotted an 'i' and turned to us. "His name is Dr. Paul Abernathy, professor emeritus of ancient languages and occult symbology from Washington State. He just retired to his estate just outside of Conifer."

"Celeste mentioned a Dr. Abernathy," I said. "She told us that he would be able to translate the ledger and the symbols around the body."

Jaw tightening again, Lance replied, "Then she's probably right. Celeste knows people." He muttered, "It's kinda her specialty."

"Then we'll go talk to him," Willow said.

Lance nodded once. "Good idea. Sainz." He pointed at the officer with his pen. "I want you to monitor the traffic cams going in and out of Conifer. See if you can find anything close to the Ravenwood Estate."

"On it, boss." Sainz got up and left the room.

"Murphy, I want you to see if you can find a connection between the vic and Morgana Ravenwood. I don't care how small of an interaction it is, just find a connection."

Murphy took a deep breath in and out, then got up and followed Sainz.

"I'm going to track down the autopsy report. See if we can glean anything from that. I'll also talk to Selena Ravenwood. She might know something we don't." Lance turned from the board to us. "We'll check in later. Good luck. I've heard the esteemed doctor can be a bit of an ass."

19

Willow

It took us nearly forty-five minutes of driving through winding forest roads to get from the police station to the Abernathy grounds. After several wrong turns, we finally found the right road. We pulled up to a large iron barred gate. As we pulled close, a tinny voice came from the access panel mounted on a goose neck pedestal in front of the gate. "Name and purpose?"

"Agent Holt, FBI," Paxton said, holding his badge to the camera on the panel. "We're here to talk to Dr. Abernathy."

There was a long pause. I continued my train of thought from the drive up. Was this case wrapped in the occult, or was someone trying to make us believe that it was? Given the history of witchcraft in the area, it would make sense for a killer to play on the suspicions of the people, especially as a means of covering their tracks. But why? Why bother with the presentation? Unless... the killer was a true practitioner of the occult.

I bit my lower lip.

There were several occult aspects to this case. I had seen similar practices in cults I had studied over the years. But the runes. Of all parts of the ritual—the staging of the body, the removal of the heart, the arrangement of the lilies—the runes made the least amount of sense to be there if it was all for show. It was possible the killer was merely theatrical as Paxton had said, but to surround the body with markings would take time and effort, especially if they weren't planned out beforehand. The repeating pattern indicated that the glyphs must have been planned. The killer must then have believed that they were important, and if they were important, they must represent something. What, then, did they represent? What ritual were they practicing?

I looked around, realizing we were still sitting in front of the gate. "Do you think he's debating letting us in?" I asked under my breath. "Or is his hired help traversing the house to find him and ask permission?"

"The latter for sure," Paxton said. "No way you can have this kind of dough and not have staff."

We continued waiting. As Paxton reached to hit the intercom button again, the iron bars in front of us pulled apart from the middle. Paxton drove through.

After passing through the gate, we made our way up a curved incline. Weeping willow trees lined the drive. The limbs had been trimmed so that only the sides of the trees furthest away from the road had hanging branches, making a kind of tunnel over the drive. A strip of sky and the road ahead were all we could make out through the trees.

"Do you think he likes willows?" Paxton asked. "Or is he trying to hide his property?"

"I was wondering the same," I replied. It took us almost ten minutes to get from the gate to the front of the house. One moment there was only road and the next, the house appeared, as if it had popped out of the ground.

The architecture of the house put in mind old British colleges. There were many stone framed windows, arches, and statues. Paxton drove onto the huge, curved cement driveway and parked in front, only a little way from the front walkway.

"Hope you're not parked in his spot," I said, and Paxton snorted as he got out of the car.

We started up the pavement. The dark covered entryway looked like the mouth of the home, open as if trying to inhale us. A marble gargoyle was perched on either side of the double wide front door, each leering at us with wide eyes and lolling tongues. In the center of both doors was a black circle knocker.

Paxton grasped the knocker on the right side and knocked three times.

A distant voice got louder and louder, as if the owner was walking closer to the door. "I'm coming, I'm coming."

The right-side door opened and man in a white three-piece suit poked his head out. "Yes, can I help you?"

"Are you Dr. Abernathy?" Paxton asked.

"I am." Abernathy pushed his half-moon spectacles up his nose. He spoke like an old gentleman. "Who are you?"

"I'm Agent Holt and this is Dr. Willow Grace. We're with the FBI. We have some questions we'd like to ask you."

Dr. Abernathy stood up straight. "In that case, you better come in."

He held the door open for us to step inside.

The entryway alone was at least as big as a normal living room. Leading from the front door to the wall opposite was a maroon runner under a line of benches pushed up against the wall. A row of empty hooks lined the wall above the bench. Large, black and white checkered tiles fanned out across the rest of the floor. A huge, curved staircase opened out to our left. A wooden lion was carved into the end of the banister. Straight ahead of us was an arched entrance to a hallway.

"Hang your coats there." Dr. Abernathy gestured to the hooks. "I'll ring for tea. Unless you prefer coffee?"

Paxton glanced at me, his face mirroring my surprise. "I—"

"I'll ask for both."

Dr. Abernathy pulled a long cloth-covered rope beside the door. A bell rang and a second later, a man in an honest-to-goodness tailcoat and white gloves appeared in the hall on the other side of the staircase.

"Bring tea and coffee to the library for our guests, if you please."

The man gave an exaggerated bow of his head before about-facing and striding off.

"This way." Dr. Abernathy gave us a polite smile and led the way down the hallway.

"I don't know what I was expecting," Paxton whispered to me. "But it certainly wasn't this."

"If only all lines of inquiry were so elegant."

We passed several oil paintings as we followed Abernathy down a long corridor where he eventually made a right turn and took a few steps down, continuing past floor to ceiling windows with an excellent view of the front lawn.

The hallway ended with another set of double doors and opened to reveal an enormous two-story room entirely lined with overflowing bookshelves.

More floor-to-ceiling windows and skylights brightened the space with the outside's overcast lighting. A wooden ladder with wheels attached to a gold rail that lined the entire room. I imagined throwing myself onto the ladder and riding the velocity of my jump for as far as it would carry me.

Several white couches and leather armchairs beckoned someone to curl up with any of the thousand old tomes around the room. A huge desk was centered almost to the back wall with a view of the whole room.

"Sit, sit, make yourselves comfortable." Dr. Abernathy pointed to a plush white couch in the middle of the floor. He sat in a leatherback chair facing the couch.

"Nice digs, Doc," Paxton said, scanning the room. "My niece is a voracious reader. She'd love this place."

I nodded. "It's beautiful."

"Why, thank you. This is my favorite room in the house, I must admit." Dr. Abernathy wore the falsely modest smile hosts do when their homes are complimented. "Now tell me, what is it that I can do for you folks?"

"We understand you are proficient in the art of translation," I said, the leatherbound journal suddenly warm against my side.

Dr. Abernathy nodded. "Depends on the subject, but I am rather fond of old, forgotten languages. So much so, I taught about them for decades at my alma mater before I retired."

"I used to be the psychology professor up at Conifer before I started working with the FBI."

"I thought I recognized your name, Dr. Grace." Dr. Abernathy smiled at me. "I have a few of your books here. Marvelous stuff. I particularly liked your newest book, *Cult Speak*."

We chatted about that for a few minutes before Paxton politely turned the conversation back to the topic at hand.

"We have something we'd like you to take a look at, Dr. Abernathy," he said. "We believe the translation of it could aid a case we're investigating."

Dr. Abernathy became grave. "You're here on account of the young lad that was found murdered this morning."

We both nodded.

"This is all the more intriguing then." The doctor sat up straight and folded his hands in his lap. "How can I help?"

20

Holt

The butler appeared in the doorway, carrying a tea-laden platter. He placed it on the coffee table between Dr. Abernathy's seat and our couch. As he leaned over, I noticed his hair was slicked back with so much product, it looked glued in place.

Abernathy leaned forward for his teacup and gestured to the butler. "Thank you, Horace, that will be all."

The butler gave a pronounced nod and left the room without a word. Dr. Abernathy then invited us to help ourselves to whichever drink we preferred.

I cleared my throat and asked, "You heard about Vyvan Wood's untimely death in the early hours of this morning?"

"Yes. It was all over town before noon, I'm sure."

I flipped to a clean page in my notebook, started tapping my pen against it. "Do you know anything about the death or crime scene?"

"No, nothing beyond him lying naked in Innocence Field."

Dr. Abernathy stirred sugar into his tea before setting his small spoon down and bringing the teacup to his lips. I wonder if the man's direct eye contact ever made his students squirm.

I also wondered how he had heard about the vic.

"That's correct," Willow said, shifting in her seat. She pulled out her phone and swiped a moment before turning it to face Abernathy. "Surrounding the body were several symbols or glyphs. Would you be able to translate these?"

Dr. Abernathy took the phone and looked at the screen over the top of his glasses. Then he held it further away and pushed his glasses up his nose. He pinched the screen to zoom in and moved his index finger in a circle across the screen, nodding his head as he stopped at each symbol.

"Yes, I believe so." Setting the phone down on the glass coffee table, he walked over to his desk. "These symbols appear to be written in Konmantic, a code from this area dated a few hundred years ago. There was an unfortunate time in Conifer's history when women weren't allowed to read or write. It was believed that it would heighten the chances of a woman becoming a witch if she could. Load of poppycock, obviously. But the women of the time came up with this code as a means of combating the laws of the time. There aren't many surviving documents now."

Willow's sour expression summed up her opinion on that bit of history. "Is this code taught in the history class at Conifer?"

"I doubt it. It's a bit too complex a code to learn given the few documents we have written in it."

Abernathy grabbed a sheet of paper and a pen from the desk and walked back over to his seat where he began to sketch a likeness to the symbols. Then he wrote something underneath each one.

"Here." He pushed the tea tray to the edge of the table and set the paper down, orienting it for us to read. He pointed to each symbol in turn. "This one means 'Innocence.' This means 'Violation.' And this last means 'Betrayal.'"

"That sounds like loads of fun," I said as Willow started rubbing her hands on her pants.

"From the way they are written out, in a triadic pattern," Abernathy said, "it looks to be part of a rite, with Innocence being the first symbol listed."

"What makes you think it's part of a rite?" Willow asked. "As opposed to something cruder, like graffiti?"

"All surviving records of witchcraft in the area list the rites they had been accused of practicing. All rites performed were done in a triadic pattern like this. The few remaining documents written in Konmantic also confirm this much."

Given that context, Vyvan had been chosen for his innocence. Celeste had described him as such. If what Dr. Abernathy said was true, then we were looking at two other victims.

"This afternoon, we acquired a notebook." I nodded to Willow, and she pulled the book from inside her jacket. "You can see by the front cover why we were interested in it."

Willow handed the book to Dr. Abernathy.

Face piqued with curiosity, the doctor set his teacup down and took the book from Willow. After running a wrinkled hand over the front cover, he unlatched the buckle and turned the cover and front page over.

"As you can see in the margins, more of the same and similar glyphs are used. Your explanation of the symbols' meanings leads me to think that the notes in the margins are also written in Konmantic," Willow said.

His eyes moved back and forth across the page for a moment before Dr. Abernathy looked up at us over his spectacles. "It certainly appears that way. Where did you acquire this?"

"Do you recognize it?" I asked.

Abernathy removed his spectacles and gestured with them, lowering his voice. "This notebook used to belong to Morgana Raven-wood. Which means you either found it in her possessions or someone close to her gave it to you.

"Since I don't detect any scent of lilies on your persons, you haven't yet been to the Ravenwood Estate. That leaves the probability of either Selena Ravenwood or Celeste Black having given you this notebook.

"As Selena Ravenwood has been notably in mourning for the past month and therefore out of the public eye, that leaves the highest likelihood of you acquiring this notebook from Miss Celeste Black." The doctor glanced between the two of us. "Am I correct?"

"Well," I started to say but Abernathy interrupted with a hearty laugh. "What a glorious day. She couldn't face me herself but she came to me for help anyways. Very like her to be so roundabout." He chuckled before growing somber as he bent over the open notebook again. "I just wish that it wasn't on account of Morgana."

Willow and I shared a brief glance. She raised her shoulder.

"I can translate this," Abernathy said, looking up. "And I will help you."

Seeing our confusion, he said, "Morgana and I used to be... very good friends. Miss Celeste never trusted me, thinking my intentions with Morgana were anything less than honest and noble. Given the unfortunate timing of when my wife left me, I could understand the confusion. However, despite, I assure you, it being entirely unrelated, Celeste believes what she wishes to believe."

He's an ass, but he knows his stuff. Celeste had said. I had to hide a snort now that I understood what she meant.

Dr. Abernathy tapped the book with a finger. "If you think that me translating this notebook will help solve the boy's murder and potentially prevent two more, if that triadic pattern is anything to go off, I will gladly do my part to help. That the notebook is in Morgana's handwriting only sweetens the interest."

"We have no idea what the notebook could contain," I said. "So, we ask that you keep it strictly between the three of us. Under penalty of obstruction of justice."

The doctor gave me a half smile. "No need to worry. Morgana was a well-loved local philanthropist. If she wrote in Konmantic, I doubt she would have wished for whatever is in this notebook to go public."

Willow set her half empty teacup down. "Thank you, Dr. Abernathy."

I put down my cup too. "Dr. Abernathy, are you aware of there being a current coven of witches in the area? Or any party or person who might practice more... extreme rituals?"

The doctor chuckled without humor. "Now that's a question you and I both would like answered, Agent Holt."

21

Willow

THE HEAVY DOOR CLOSED WITH A THUD BEHIND US AS WE walked back to our parked car.

"Do you think he really cheated on his wife with Morgana?" Paxton asked as he unlocked the car doors.

"Would make sense why Celeste doesn't like him." I slipped into the car. I had to wonder why Celeste hadn't been equally displeased with Morgana though. "We should call Lance."

"Read my mind." Paxton connected his phone to the car and started driving.

The dial-out tone chimed over the car speakers. The huge manor's silhouette merged with encroaching twilight in the sideview mirror before Paxton turned the corner into the weeping willow tunnel. He pressed a button on the center dash and warm air blew from the air vents, heating my skin. Our headlights reflected dimly off the leaves as we moved forward, brightening the tunnel as we drove back down to the gate.

After a handful of rings, Lance answered. "Holt, what's going on?"

"Just finished interviewing Dr. Abernathy," Paxton replied.

"He agreed to translate the ledger for us," I said.

Lance made a noise of approval. "That's excellent. What else did he say? Was he able to translate the symbols by the body?"

"Yes." I pulled the paper out of my pocket and unfolded it before launching into a quick recap of our conversation that afternoon. We pulled to a stop at the gate, now lit by several lights on top of its tall markers. The iron bars slowly opened from the middle.

"You're saying, then, that we might be looking at two more possible victims?"

"Yes. How are things going on your end?" I asked.

"Not so well," Lance admitted. "The soonest we'll get the autopsy report is next week. In the meantime, I tried to get ahold of Selena Ravenwood, but I couldn't find her. She didn't answer any of my calls and she didn't answer when I knocked on her door. I'll have to try again tomorrow."

The gate finished rolling open with a light squeal, the metal rocking slightly from the sudden halt.

"We want to head to the Ravenwood Estate," Paxton said, now driving forward. "It's the logical next step with how Morgana Ravenwood seems to be in the middle of everything."

"I agree." Lance sighed. "But it's late. Best save it for tomorrow."

"Sure thing." I stifled a yawn as I answered. "We'll see you in the morning."

"No need to check in beforehand," Lance told us. "Just head straight to the Ravenwood Estate and you can update me after."

Paxton glanced at me to confirm before saying, "Will do," and ending the call.

Just as he hung up, the phone rang loud from the Bluetooth speakers.

"It's Cannonball," Paxton said, referring to our boss with the nickname Del had given him. "Hey," he answered. "Willow's here, too."

"Excellent," McCannon replied. "Wanted to check in with you guys. How're you doing?"

Paxton gave him the rundown of events from today.

McCannon was quiet for a moment. I imagined him drilling the table top with his fingers. "You think that this is an offshoot of the Rendezvous case?"

"I do," Paxton said. "We'll know better when we get the autopsy report, but Lance said it could take a week."

McCannon made a noncommittal noise. "What do you think, Grace?"

I thought for a moment, watching the road ahead. "I'm not convinced. There are anomalies that don't line up with the ring's MO. I mean for one, we have a body. We're still missing at least a dozen in the Rendezvous case. Second, there are just too many theatrics." I explained my thoughts about the runes. "That's just too out of nowhere for the ring."

"What Willow says makes sense," Paxton said. "I can't deny that. But it's also strange to me that the organ removal process on Vyvan Woods is exactly the same as what we discovered on Baily's body, down to identical lacerations."

"Yes," I conceded. "But maybe he was inspired by the Rendezvous case."

Paxton's nostrils flared as he said, "Or they're connected."

"Don't fill in gaps with presuppositions, Holt." McCannon's voice took on an edge.

I put a placating hand on Paxton's arm as he started to huff. "Maybe you're right. I'm just not convinced yet."

There was a small pause.

"I see," McCannon eventually said. "Keep me posted."

Paxton nodded at the car speaker. "Will do, sir."

"And Grace, you have a message."

Who would send me a message via McCannon? "From who?"

"Kincaid."

I looked at Paxton, his brows furrowed.

"What did he say?" I asked.

"He said, and I quote, 'Innocence is precious simply because it's fleeting. It would be a shame if what you'd buried were violated, wouldn't it, little Miss Peirce?'"

My chest constricted, the hairs on the back of my neck prickling. I felt more than watched the car jerk to the side of the road and pull to a stop. Paxton's hand was on my shoulder, the other grabbing my clenched fist in my lap.

"Given the update you all just gave me, this message seems too on the nose for Kincaid to be playing coy. Why would Kincaid want to give you such a message, Grace? I take it the name Peirce is significant to you?"

"Used to be," I murmured, thoughts reeling. McCannon remained silent, waiting for an explanation.

Voice shaking, I asked, "When did he give you this message?"

"Earlier today." McCannon waited a moment more, but I was unable to put any thought into words.

He took pity on me. "Let me know what you think it means after you've had time to think about it. I'll expect to hear from you tomorrow."

"Yes, sir," Paxton responded and disconnected the phone. He rubbed my shoulder and took my other hand in his palm. "Are you okay?"

I squeezed his hand tighter but didn't reply.

"He used 'innocence' and 'violated' in the same sentence," he said.

I nodded. "I caught that."

"This is Kincaid we're talking about." I turned my gaze to face Paxton. His eyes were kind, but his face was set. "That can't be coincidental."

I nodded again. "I agree."

I sat in silence, *Little Miss Peirce* repeating in my mind. What could he mean? If what I had buried was violated... was he referring to my past? The cultish hell I had escaped? Innocence, precious, fleeting...

Little Miss Peirce. He couldn't have meant...

The possibility I most wanted yet most feared played out in my mind.

"I'm sorry he used your old name." Paxton squeezed my arm, his touch jolting me back to the present. "I hope that wasn't too upsetting for you."

"That's just it though." I bit my lip, putting my hand over his. "I don't... I know it's crazy, but I don't actually think he was referring to me. I still don't know how he knows my old last name, but he said *Little Miss* Peirce. He's never referred to me that way."

I rubbed my now-sweating palms against my thighs to stop my hands from shaking. "What if he's referring to Winnie?"

"Winnie?" Paxton's eyebrows rose. "How does Winnie fit into this?"

"What if... what if knows where she is?"

Paxton tilted his head, almost shaking it. "Willow, I'm not tracking here."

"Kincaid knew all about Winnie. He knew the hell she escaped from and that she went into Witness Protection."

"And because of that cryptic message, you think he knows where she is?" Paxton furrowed his brows. "Willow, that's not possible. She's gone. No one will ever see her again, not with how good our protection programs are. Least of all Kincaid since he's in prison."

"I know." I chewed my lip harder, a metallic tang forming on my tongue. "Like always, he's leaving me in the dark. He only ever gives me enough to just ask more questions. But this? This doesn't make sense. But why cushion that message with the rest of the riddle?" I slumped back, thumping my head against the head rest. "What does anything have to do with—with anything?"

"I love it when you speak in a circle. Super easy to follow."

I turned my head to glare at him. "Ha, ha."

Paxton chuckled before turning serious again. "I know this is frustrating. Maybe that message is about Winnie, but I doubt it. Even if it is, we have to keep our sights on *this* case right now. We can look more into 'anything about anything' once we've caught this killer." He put his hand on my face, cupping my cheek. "Alright?"

I didn't lean into his touch. "I know you're right but finding out what Kincaid's playing at is important to me, especially if it involves Winnie. Please, trust my gut on this. And I'll try to be more open-minded about the trafficking connection."

Paxton stiffened at my words, before relaxing. "Deal."

I leaned into his touch then. "Witches first."

Then we could worry about Winnie.

22

Willow

As Paxton drove us to Ravenwood Estate the next morning, my eyes were bleary and unfocused. Caffeine and dulling adrenaline served as my only fuel as I hadn't slept well the night before. The cold, wet morning did nothing to help the groggy tightness around my skull. Solid clouds blocked any sunlight, and large drops of rain plopped onto our windshield as we passed under the trees by the road, indicating it had rained the night before.

After fifteen minutes of winding through pothole-riddled backroads, we pulled onto a small drive to the Ravenwood Estate. Despite my time spent in Conifer, I had never been here. I'd only seen photos or heard of it in passing. Most of the photos of the place were from news articles written about the events that Morgana had sometimes hosted. She'd mainly host the town's council board, socialites, local politicians, school board members and the like. I had been invited to one such event, but after learning that it was favored to be nationally publicized due to the guestlist, I had opted not to attend, still afraid of my past finding me.

We slowed to a stop in front of a tall iron gate. A thick vine hung over the swirling metal and curled around to its stone enclosure. The gate was ajar, an open invitation for trespassers.

"I don't think it's supposed to be open, do you?" Paxton asked.

I shook my head. "Don't think so. Especially not after Celeste's comment about trespassers."

Paxton got out of the car and walked closer to the gate. I followed him, shutting the car door with a soft thud. My shoes padded against the uneven weed-covered ground. I side-stepped the potholes approaching the gate.

"I wonder if we came the right way? For a lady as wealthy as Morgana, this isn't well maintained. Maybe this is a back entrance?"

"Maybe." Paxton tapped the side of his leg as he craned his neck up towards the gate and nodded. "Hey, look at this."

I stepped closer, craning my neck and squinting. Lichen and rust had corroded the iron. It opened one way, from left to right, on a metal rolling mechanism. The gate arched at the top and contained a symbol in the middle. The same symbol on the front of Morgana's ledger.

Paxton turned from the gate to me. "Coincidences are not to be trusted."

I got my phone out and took a picture of the gate, a niggling feeling starting down my spine. *Gates often led to more questions than answers.*

"Think we should try to go forward, or find another entrance? Maybe we should—"

The crunching of dirt and gravel under tires had us turning around.

A gray Audi pulled up behind us, centered in the small drive. A tall woman with long, curled hair got out and slammed her door behind her. Her black business suit was fitted to her slender body. The only color on her were her red lips and matching red nails. The scent of perfume became stronger as she stormed towards us. There was something familiar about it, but the woman started talking before I could put my finger on why.

"Who are you?" the woman growled at us. Closer now, the bags under her eyes were evident. "This is private property. Clear out."

"We're not here to cause problems, ma'am." Paxton stepped forward, pulling out his badge and holding it up. "Agent Holt, FBI, here for Ms. Selena Ravenwood."

"My grandmother's death was ruled an accident." The woman looked between us for a moment, a heaviness pulling her shoulders forward. "Can't you let her rest?"

"So you're Selena Ravenwood?" Paxton asked. She nodded, folding her arms. "We're very sorry for your loss. But we're not here to ask questions regarding your grandmother's death. We want to see your gardens."

Selena blinked. "Our gardens?"

"I assume they belong to you now? May we see them?"

"Yes, I-I suppose you're right." Tears formed in Selena's eyes. "I don't live on the estate, but I was driving this way to check the mail. Few people even know this back entrance exists, so you can understand my surprise when I saw fresh tracks."

Paxton nodded. "Certainly. That would give me pause, too."

"The gardens are on the north side of the property, about four miles from here. But I can take you in to see them. Do you have a warrant?"

Paxton's jaw tightened. "No, but we will go get one, if that's a problem."

Selena shook her head, eyes on the gate. "No, it's fine. Let's just get this over with." She started walking towards her car when she turned to us again. "Was the gate open when you got here?"

I nodded. "Yes. We didn't go through."

Selena gave a tiny nod, her gaze on the gate again. She got in her car and did a four point turn back around. She idled in the drive, backlights lit, waiting for us to follow. Paxton and I got back in our car and followed her down the bumpy drive.

About twenty minutes later, we approached the main entrance of the Ravenwood Estate. The drive was paved smooth to the wide iron double gate. Selena didn't bother driving to the goose neck panel. The gate opened from the side automatically. Maybe she had a remote in her car.

We drove through behind her. The Ravenwood Estate was much greener and somehow darker than the Abernathy grounds. There was less open lawn and far more trees. As the house, a glorious Victorian style manor home, came into view I noticed that the tops of trees were poking out of the roof, as if the house had been built around a small grove.

I pointed to the trees. "Morgana must have had terrible foundation problems."

Paxton leaned forward to see the roof better. "No kidding. It's beautiful though."

Selena parked in front of a four-car garage built on the side of the home and got out. Paxton pulled in next to her and we followed suit. The air smelled of rain and wet plants. A small gust of wind followed Selena as she walked over to us, catching her hair and blowing it about her face.

"Welcome to Ravenwood." Her tone was polite, but her expression had no liveliness in it. Even her dark eyes were like the darkness of a forgotten well. "I didn't catch your names earlier?"

We introduced ourselves and I murmured a greeting.

Selena inclined her head. "I've heard of you two. I wish we could have met under more pleasurable circumstances." She turned to Paxton. "You said you needed to see my grandmother's gardens?"

"We believe it might hold some clues to help us with a case." Paxton took out his notebook. "A college student was found dead in Innocence Field yesterday morning. His body was surrounded by flowers. As far as we know, your grandmother's garden is the only place with said flowers actively growing."

Selena's eyes widened, her breathing hitched. "Someone was found dead? Why haven't I heard of this? Who was it?"

"A young man named Vyvan Woods," I said. It seemed strange that she hadn't heard about it before now. I wondered why Celeste hadn't said anything to her, or if the two of them didn't have a close relationship.

Selena let out a small though sharp exhale. "That's terrible. That was Celeste's young man, wasn't it?"

Paxton frowned. "What do you mean?"

"I mean—" Selena shook her head. "I mean he got the county's scholarship, right?"

"That's right."

"I wonder if she saw him last..." Selena shook her head again. "Let me lead you to the green houses."

She turned and walked past the garage doors onto a small, sectioned stone pathway that looped behind the garage.

The pathway led to several greenhouses. Sunlight illuminated the inside, condensation on the walls sparkling. Selena walked up to the first greenhouse in a line of three, took out her keys, and unlocked an old-fashioned iron lock.

"You keep your greenhouses locked?" Paxton asked.

"We've been having trouble with trespassers lately. Some thought my grandmother was a witch." Selena pushed open the door and stepped inside to hold the door open. "They come for a cheap thrill."

"We've heard that rumor," I said as I stepped in.

"It's insufferable. After all the good my grandmother did for the community and yet still people whisper behind her back." Selena stepped to the side and turned to face us.

The humid air inside warmed my skin, thawing out the chill that had seeped into my fingers. In the roughly twenty feet by sixteen feet space were a dozen raised flower beds, six on each side flush against the walls creating a walkway down the middle, leading to another door.

Closing my eyes, I took a deep breath of the air and caught a very faint scent of lilies. I opened them and looked at each of the beds. Some held sprouts, while others overflowed with flowers or small bushes.

"What was the flower you were looking for, specifically?" Selena asked.

Paxton began answering when my phone started buzzing in my pocket. Dr. Abernathy's name lit up the caller ID. I held up a finger to Paxton and Selena and they both nodded. I walked towards the entrance of the greenhouse, my back facing them.

"Hello? Dr. Abernathy?"

"Dr. Grace! Good morning." His polite tone was filled with excitement. "Is now a good time?"

"As good as any. What's up? Have you found something?"

"Yes, I think I have. I'm not quite halfway done with my translation, but I have enough to perhaps point you and Agent Holt in the right direction."

My heart beat faster. "That's excellent news!"

"Can you come now?"

I tracked Paxton making his way up the line of beds, scrutinizing each plant in turn. "We're in the middle of something right now, but we can come over as soon as we're done."

"Splendid. Horace will open the gate for you."

"Thanks Doctor, we'll see you soon." I hung up.

"What was in this bed?" Paxton asked from the other side of the greenhouse.

Selena, who had been watching me, turned and walked over to where Paxton was standing, her brow furrowing. I followed and saw that the bed was devoid of any plants, as though the dirt was all recently tilled. A single white petal poked out of the earth.

"This was where my grandmother had planted the Asiatic White lilies." She pointed to the name that had been written in gold lettering on the front of the flower bed. "But they're all gone," she raised the tone of the last word into a question.

"So we see," Paxton said.

"I-I don't know how, we keep these gardens under lock and key." Selena blinked at the bare beds, her body stiff and frozen. "But I haven't been out here in weeks."

"Does anyone else have access to these greenhouses?" I asked.

Selena ran her tongue across her teeth, her brows now pinched. "The grounds keeper and the gardener. And... Celeste, I think."

"Were these all the lilies?" I asked. "Or are more planted anywhere else?"

"There might be more in the other greenhouses." Selena turned to unlock the second door with another key. But it was already open. "What—"

She pushed the door wide and stepped onto the interconnecting pathway. The sound of a metal lock clanking against glass sounded and Selena hesitated. "This one's unlocked too."

She pushed in and clasped a hand to her mouth after a sharp intake of breath.

Paxton pushed her to the side and grunted. Several of the raised beds had been pushed over, dirt scattered all over the floor.

"Our staff would never leave a greenhouse in a state like this," Selena whispered.

Paxton turned back to Selena. "Do you have any security cameras? Anything that tracks who might have come in here?"

As she shook her head and explained that there weren't any cameras on the property, I took a step back onto the pathway, thinking.

If this was where the lilies had been acquired, that greatly limited the suspect pool. I turned to my left to see an open field, with a thick parameter of trees surrounding it. In the center was a large monument, clearly brand new, judging by the lack of lichen and how white the stone was.

Except that what once must have been a majestic stone lion was now a headless body overlooking a freshly dug and broken grave.

23

Willow

"Selena?" I said, unable to look away from the broken monument. "Was that your grandmother's grave?"

"What do you mean 'was'?" The tall woman poked her head out of the greenhouse and followed my line of sight. Her face turned stark white.

She stepped out of the greenhouse and sprinted across the grass to the monument despite her five-inch stilettos. Paxton and I ran after her. A second later I came up, panting, and looked at the wreckage.

The monument was made up of a life size lion on its stone perch. Its head lay on the ground next to the base, its mouth open and mournful, the neck severed as if it had been ripped clean off its body. The words *A Beating Heart Proves There Is More to Life Than Mere Blood* were carved onto a stone slab, cracked at the top corner.

Selena's breaths were shaky and ragged. Tears poured down her cheeks.

"Selena?" I reached out to touch her. When the tips of my fingers brushed her skin, she fell to the ground, sobbing. I sank down and put an arm around her.

My body shook with her sobs and tears formed in my own eyes. I'd heard of people desecrating graves before, but to see it in person was sobering in a way I'd never imagined. Adjusting so that Selena's head was cradled on my shoulder, I looked back down at the grave.

The same three symbols that surrounded Vyvan's body were drawn underneath in red, the middle one having been drawn the largest and thickest. Red petals, so dark they were almost black, littered the whole area like blood-colored confetti.

Paxton pulled out his phone, pressed a button, and held it up to his ear. "Lance? Get down to the Ravenwood Estate immediately. We found something."

Selena pulled herself away from my embrace, crawling to the edge of a gaping hole in front of the monument. Her face paled at the sight of an open wood coffin. She screamed and nearly fell in. I grabbed her, pulled her away from the hole when the unmistakable smell of decomposition wafted into my nose.

Morgana Ravenwood lay in the coffin, hands crossed over her abdomen. She might have looked peaceful, if she hadn't been some three weeks decayed. A hole had been carved out where her heart should have been.

About twenty minutes later Lance arrived with a team. Wind had picked up as we waited, now toying with our hair and the edges of our clothes.

I was still holding Selena, now a few paces further back from the broken grave. At one point I had suggested we go inside but she had shaken her head. Black lines streaked her face and mascara caked under her eyes.

"Who would do this?" she whispered between sobs and gulps for air. "Who would do this?"

After Lance had set a perimeter, instructing his men to take pictures and document the entire site, Paxton gave him a rundown of everything since we had arrived. I had coaxed Selena to the base of some trees not too far from the grave. One of the team members came over to ask us standard procedural questions. Selena finally agreed to go inside when that team member suggested they get her a glass of water.

After receiving a promise from the officer that they would keep an eye on Selena, I squeezed her shoulder one last time and walked back to the desecrated grave.

The symbols drew me in like a trainwreck. I stepped on a few stray petals as I came closer, their soft skin ripping under my feet. Once I got to the edge of the grave, I pulled out my phone and the paper from Dr. Abernathy to compare the glyphs to that of the first crime scene. In the dirt around the grave, the second symbol in the triadic pattern was carved bigger than the other two.

Violation.

That was what the second symbol meant.

"Find something?" Lance asked.

I nodded and handed him the paper. "This was the initial translation that Dr. Abernathy did for us. The middle one is exaggerated this time, the symbol meaning violation."

Lance scanned the paper and the stone slab. "This grave and body have been violated alright."

"This doesn't make any sense," Paxton said. "The MO isn't the same. This isn't a new—fresh—victim." He picked up a red petal and inspected it. "We don't even have whole flowers this time."

He was right. The similarities were there, but the differences were stark enough to give me pause.

Paxton let the petal float to the earth. "Why on earth would you harvest a half-decomposed heart?"

Lance handed the paper back to me. "This being a rite or a ritual is sounding more and more plausible."

"I just don't understand why," I said. "If a ritual *is* being performed, what's its purpose?"

"Anything come up while we've been here?" Paxton asked Lance. "Sainz find anything from the security cameras?"

"A gray Audi was recorded driving away from the Ravenwood Estate yesterday, late afternoon."

We all exchanged a look. Celeste and Selena both had gray Audis.

"How?" I asked. "Selena told us there were no cameras on the estate."

"And as far as we know, she's right," Lance said. "There is, however, a city camera at the end of the drive towards the back of her property. Morgana commissioned it. Claimed it was for insurance reasons."

Why would Morgana commission a camera there?

"How far back in the footage did Sainz search?" Paxton asked.

"Unfortunately, it self-deletes footage every forty-eight hours," Lance said.

"Sir! Sheriff!" Murphy, who had simultaneously been turning more and more green as he stood by the tomb taking pictures, stood straight up. "Sir, there's another note."

"Where?"

"Same as last time."

Lance walked over to Murphy who handed him a pair of gloves. He knelt by Morgana's head, pulled a folded piece of paper from behind her ear, and opened it. Paxton and I leaned forward over the corner of the grave. The smell of rotting flesh caught my nostrils again.

He lifted the note in my direction. "It's labeled for you, Dr. Grace."

My heart skipped a beat as he stepped out of the grave.

After I pulled on a pair of gloves, Lance handed me the note. He then stepped back and pulled out his phone. Paxton leaned over my shoulder, close enough for me to smell his aftershave as I looked down at the writing, noting it was the same kind of paper and the handwriting looked the same as the short, cryptic first note: "Listen to her." At the top of the list was a set of numbers.

Dr. Grace, find me here. I know who killed Morgana and I know who's going to die next. Bring only Agent Holt.

Paxton tapped on the line of numbers. "Those are coordinates."

"Not too far from here, actually." Lance lowered his phone and pointed towards the woods. "Somewhere in that direction if this map can be trusted."

"Someone had to have placed the note in the grave after it was broken into," Paxton said, his tone clipped. "The person who wrote it might have seen who did this."

"We should go," I said. "Right now."

Lance raised a halting hand. "I can't just let you run off. How do we know this wasn't written by the killer? What if it's a trap?"

"True," I said. "But how do we know it's *not* written by someone who's trying to help us?"

"Then we'll all go, and my team will be back up," Lance said.

"That specifically goes against the instructions of the note. Who's to say they won't see us coming and refuse to talk to us if the whole calvary comes?" I folded the note back up. "We should go now, while the weather's still dry."

We all glanced at the sky. The gray cloud cover was darkening by the minute.

"You'll need to get the grave covered before it rains anyways," I said.

Lance looked like he wanted to keep arguing but he turned to Paxton instead. "What do you think about this?"

Paxton regarded me. "Willow's gut is telling us to go, so we need to go." He faced Lance. "Always goes badly when we don't listen to Willow's gut."

Lance sighed and waved his hand. "Fine." He turned to his team and shouted, "Someone bring me Gertha Mae, stat."

24

Willow

According to Lance's map, the coordinates led through the woods a couple miles out. He suggested a UTV could be the best way to get us there. Within the hour, after Paxton and I geared up with vests, radios, maps, and an honest-to-goodness compass, the thunder of a large engine reverberated through the clearing. A large, gray, UTV with an impressive roll cage and storage rack on the back came barreling to where we were stationed by the edge of the tree line.

It pulled to a stop and Davis, the young rookie we had met at the first crime scene, hopped out. He threw the keys to Lance.

He caught them and patted the hood of the vehicle. "Meet Gertha Mae."

Even despite the seriousness of the situation, my ribs constricted in amusement at the look of delight on Paxton's face.

"She'll get you anywhere in half the time with twice the finesse as any other UTV out there." He threw the keys at Paxton. "Helmets should be in the back. Let's get you rolling."

And three minutes after that, Paxton behind the wheel, we were driving through the acres of Ravenwood's estate forest. We were quiet most of the way as he drove. He followed a beaten path, little more than a deer trail, for the first mile. The deeper we drove, the more we had to forge our way through the underbrush.

"I wonder if we're still on Ravenwood property," Paxton said to me, having to nearly yell over the sound of the engine.

I tried to shrug, though the bumpiness of the ride made it hard. "Beats me. I wouldn't be surprised though."

"We seem to traverse through forests a lot for cases."

"I was thinking that. It's like Marlborough all over again."

"Hopefully this time we won't find human remains by an altar and a get attacked by a crazy homeless dude."

I laughed and Paxton kept driving.

We came onto a small clearing. Paxton slowed to the edge of the trees, and we peered at the field of tall grass with a now empty dry mound in the center of it. A stray line of police tape flapped from one of the trees on the other side of the field.

"This is Innocence Field."

Paxton raised his brow. "You're right."

"I guess this answers whether we're still on the Estate."

Paxton grunted in acknowledgment and pointed at the map in my hands. "We veered too far west."

"Wait." I handed him the map and hopped out of the UTV, walking towards the tree line to something that glinted through the foliage on the ground.

"What is it?" Holt asked, shouting over the engine.

I stooped beside a tall clump of grass and pushed some of the stalks to the side. Having found what had been glinting, I stood and held it for Paxton to see.

It was a pair of glasses.

I looked up to the field again, something about standing here niggling at my memory. Flipping the glasses over, I walked through the memory again. After a few seconds, it clicked: there had been a figure standing in the trees yesterday morning, watching the police proceedings.

I walked back to the UTV and twirled the glasses in my fingers. "They were half hidden in a clump of tall grass."

Paxton frowned at the glasses in my hand. "Odd place for a pair of glasses, huh?"

I nodded and told him about what I had seen yesterday morning.

"Why didn't you say anything about it?"

"Because when I looked again, whoever it was was already gone. I was worried I had just imagined it."

Paxton furrowed his brows but nodded. "Can't say that I wouldn't have done the same thing."

He waited for me to tuck the glasses into my jacket pocket and strap in again before handing me back the map, turning around, and heading north.

An old green bicycle rested against a tree ahead of us, glinting in the speckled sunlight.

"Slow down," I shouted, pointing at the bike. "Look at that."

Paxton slowed and I got a closer look at the cycle. The body of the bike shone as if recently washed. Despite its current home in the forest, the wheels were free of dirt and debris.

Paxton killed the engine. "What's that doing way out here?"

"And why is it spotless?"

Paxton pulled off his helmet, took the map and compass from me, and got out of the UTV. I followed and came up beside him as he consulted the map next to the bike. "We're almost right on top of the coordinates."

I looked at the trees around us before turning my gaze to the ground. A small distance ahead of where the bike was leaning against the trunk was a small indent in the ground. "Look," I said. "Is that a—"

"Footprint?" Paxton crouched down, pulling out a flashlight and pointing it at the ground. "Looks like it."

The ground was still dry from the last few days of unexpected spring weather, but the rain in the night had started moistening the forest floor. More footsteps led through the brush and greenery. We followed them until we came to a tight bundle of trees. Two large ones stood arm's length apart having intertwined branches above our heads that made the space between them appear as a kind of doorway.

Paxton and I exchanged a glance before I pulled out my phone and took a picture of the symbols. Paxton pulled out his gun and made his way forward. We walked through a small tunnel of trees to a tiny alcove.

A rectangular tarp had been erected with ropes and bungee cords around the four trunks. A bed roll and multiple blankets were piled on top of a mound of moss and ferns underneath. Dark, wrinkled clothing spilled out of a worn duffle bag in the corner.

"Hello?" Paxton called out.

"This is Dr. Willow Grace and Agent Holt," I said. "It sounds like you can answer some questions for us?"

A man's brittle voice with a British accent sounded from nearby. "Put that gun away, fool, lest you make the forest angry."

I gasped and tensed, while Paxton looked around, still holding his gun up.

"I said put it away." The voice came from the back of the alcove.

A withered hand wrapped around a small tree trunk. An eye peeped out from the side. Half a face peered out from behind the trunk. The person was old and androgynous, with long greasy white hair hanging in curtains everywhere.

"I don't want guns here," he said.

Paxton hesitated but holstered his gun and held up his empty hands. "We got a note with these coordinates. Did you write it?"

"Of course I did," the man said. "Do you think the pixies wrote it? Come a little closer, my eyes aren't as keen without my glasses."

"You mean these?" I reached for the glasses I had found and walked slowly towards him, holding them out. "Are these yours?"

"You found them, bless you! Please give them to me!"

He swiped them out of my hand and stepped behind the tree to put them on before sticking his head out again, further this time. Now I caught a glimpse of a long and bulbous nose, with a mole right on the end.

"Thank you for finding them."

"You're welcome," I said hesitantly before gesturing behind me to Paxton. "You know who we are. Who are you?"

"I am the Keeper of Knowledge." He stepped out further, bowing his head in greeting. "But you can call me Kay."

25

Four weeks ago...

Morgana Ravenwood

Morgana couldn't stand it.

She stopped at the accent table, willing the soft touch of her lily petals to ease her inner turmoil. When that didn't work, she peered out the floor-to-ceiling windows to her greenhouses on the lawn. But the serenity of the view had as little affect as the lilies.

It was mid-afternoon and the day was unseasonably warm. On any other day, she would be able to see her gardeners tending the greenhouses or the landscaping around the deck, but today the yard was empty. Barren of bodies.

She hadn't heard from Jim. It was shipment day. The little toad was never late and always, *always* checked in ahead of time. So where was he?

She began pacing the room again, reaching her mind into the ether. There was something different, a subtle change in the energy of the world. There weren't as many threads of consciousness, mortal lifelines, connected to Conifer. Why? What had changed? She reached her hand deep into her pocket and fiddled the clasp of her leatherbound ledger. Perhaps this was a sign. The energies of the earth were moving her to this decision. Her knees quaked beneath her. She wasn't ready to face Gum and yet the longer she waited, the more innocent blood was on her head.

She'd never intended to hurt anyone. The laws that governed her people wouldn't allow it, but she knew better. She knew that, rather than live by the laws her very station represented, she had chosen her own life over countless others.

Morgana couldn't do it anymore.

She was old now, older than she ever should have been. Pressing her fingers to her right pectoral, she traced the old scar through her clothes. Each beat of her heart was a precious, stolen commodity. Each beat put her further in debt.

A weight fell on her mind, the beginnings of a premonition. Morgana stilled, then turned on the TV in the corner, hoping the premonition would result in either dispelling her nervous energy or finding the source of her worry.

A large man with salt and pepper hair at a press conference appeared on the screen. *Trafficking Ring Dismantled Earlier This Afternoon* flashed across the bottom of the screen. Morgana sucked in a breath.

"Director McCannon, is this the fastest solved case of organ trafficking on record?" a newscaster asked.

"I can't speak to that," said McCannon. "But I do know that if it weren't for my team, this never would have been possible and many more lives would have been lost."

"Has the infamous organ trafficker Jim Gum been arrested?"

"We have him in custody now."

The remote slipped through Morgana's fingers and she crumpled to the floor.

Jim Gum had been arrested.

She was free.

Morgana walked on clouds all week. Even the growing pains in her chest couldn't lower her spirit. She was a bird finally freed from its cage, a bee allowed to pollinate after a long winter. But even as light as she felt, that old pain was growing in her chest again. She needed to make some tinctures to alleviate the worsening symptoms, so she dropped by the Apothecary one week after she had watched the press conference.

"Ma'am!" Cynthia had exclaimed as Morgana waltzed through the employees' entrance. "I wasn't expecting to see you today."

"It's quite alright Cynthia, nothing to worry about." Morgana put on an apron and started gathering ingredients from around the back employee kitchen. "I had a free afternoon, so I figured I'd come help whip up the cordials for the summit this weekend. Plus I have a few tinctures I wanted to experiment with and an observance to put together."

Cynthia's frowned, the light catching her eyes accentuated by dark makeup. "That's beneath your station, ma'am."

"I must say you look exquisite, my dear. But this is how I plan to spend my afternoon." She batted her hand in the door's direction. "Run along."

Cynthia, as if compelled, nodded and took her own apron off. She gave Morgana another look before retreating to the storefront.

Over the course of the afternoon, Morgana worked, throwing herself into the privilege of getting to work instead of overseeing another one of those ghastly shipments. At one point she overheard Cynthia talking on the phone and, from her side of the conversation,

Morgana guessed it was her most recent lover. It sounded as if she was apologizing for being late.

"Yes, do let her know. It's entirely my fault, I've lost track of the time. I have to dash now, goodbye, my dear Malley."

More time passed, Morgana lost in the joy of working with her hands. To experiment with concoctions, to use the remains of foraged ingredients was a delight on which she had long since missed out. The bell over the front door jingled. By the sudden warmth and pheromones she could sense even from here, she guessed it was Cynthia's lover. She had been wanting to meet him, pleased that one of her dear children was happy.

Morgana listened to the two of them chatting before footsteps announced Cynthia's return to the employee kitchen.

"My dear Malcolm is here." Cynthia's eyes were bright. "I don't suppose you'd come out and meet him?"

Morgana laughed. "Of course, my dear," she said, and the chiming of the bells above the front door rang out again. "You go on out. I'll be out in a moment."

Cynthina left and as Morgana took her apron off, she sensed a much more guarded presence at the shop front. A woman with deep scars and several unresolved queries plaguing her mind.

Morgana approached the front of the shop. Cynthia introduced her to Malcolm Baldor, as wonderful a man as Cynthia had ever described, and the famous Dr. Willow Grace, an alert and pretty woman wearing a puffy coat and guarded expression behind the polite smile on her face.

As the four of them chatted, Morgana watched Dr. Grace as a weight pressed on her mind again, a new premonition forming. The image that formed in her mind's eye was murky, clouded with pain and heartbreak. As plagued as this woman was now, her future was fraught with more questions and uncertainties.

"Well, now my children, I have kept you from your engagement far longer than I should have. Run along now. I'll lock up behind you, Cynthia, dear. Again, a pleasure to meet both of you."

Morgana walked back behind the counter, before stopping in the doorway, the premonition sharpening into clear focus. She turned back to see the doctor putting on her gloves by the front entrance. "Dr. Grace?"

The woman looked up, a strand of brown falling from her ponytail to the side of her face.

"I sense you'll find her. But not in the way you would ever expect. Look out for the nine-fingered man."

Morgana smiled and went to the back of the shop, her heart throbbing against her sternum.

Even as the pain grew and the storm that had been threatening all day finally came pouring down in buckets, all was right in Morgana's world until she arrived back home. As much as her granddaughter teased her for keeping a landline, Morgana insisted on having one. As soon as she had taken off her coat and hung it on one of the branches of the tree in the foyer, she went into her study to see the light flashing on the phone port. she pressed the button to listen.

"So sorry to call you so late, Morgana." That familiar voice sent a chill down her spine. "I'm sure you saw the news report. Rest assured that everything is going exactly as planned. We actually have a new order of operation coming into effect. We'll be sending a representative to your home tomorrow morning to work out the finer details of your new contract. Stand by for instructions. You know the consequences if you don't." And the line disconnected.

Morgana sank into her seat, her entire body shaking. Sobs threatened to erupt, and her chest burned with the force to keep them at bay. She rubbed a fist against her forehead. She should have known.

She cried out to the ether, and the energies of the earth flowed into her. Morgana wouldn't form a new contract. She wouldn't allow more innocents to be discarded, burned, and buried on her property again. Never again.

She patted her side, the ledger tucked safely in the folds of her deepest pocket.

But at the sporadic rhythm of her heart, she realized her treasured journal was no longer safe with her. The secret insurance she had been compiling for years needed a new home.

26

Recognition hit me like a ton of bricks. "You're Kay?"

"Morgana sometimes referred to me as her bookkeeper." Kay grinned, half of his face still blocked by the tree trunk. "But I am much, much more than that."

I inclined my head. "It's nice to meet you, Kay."

"Likewise, Dr. Grace." He jumped a little and looked from side to side. "Were you two followed?"

"Not as far as we know," Paxton said. "We didn't see anyone else."

Kay's eye moved to Paxton. "Would you promise that, Agent Holt?"

Paxton raised his eyebrows. "Of course."

Kay took a step from behind the tree, his squat figure wrapped in a cloak. The hood was tucked behind his long, tattered white hair. Billowing sleeves enveloped his gnarled, withered hands.

"Good," he said, stepping in front of the tree and taking a seat on the ground

He patted the ground, gesturing for us to join him. A stain marred the cloth on his left shoulder. Kay rolled up his sleeves, revealing welts and cuts covering his skin.

Seating myself in a lotus position, dampness from the ground seeping into the seat of my pants. Paxton dropped to a low crouch beside me.

"What happened to you?" I asked, nodding at Kay's arms.

Kay looked down, splaying his palms in front of him, then looking at the backs of his hands. "Oh, this. I was merely chased and left for dead." Upon seeing my expression, he said, "It's not the first time that's happened to me, I can assure you."

"What happened to you?" Paxton asked.

The man shook his head. "Doesn't matter. In the end it was my own blasted foolishness."

"That's a pretty big stain. Were you stabbed or shot?"

Kay shook his head again, though his hand had jumped up to his shoulder.

I leaned forward and brought his attention back to me. "You said you know who killed Morgana?"

Kay lowered his head and said in a slight singsong, "I do and so should you."

Paxton shifted his weight. "Did you see who broke into Morgana's grave?"

Kay's expression darkened. "That is a sacrilege that never should have taken place, our poor matriarch." Tears poured down his face as he put his head between his legs, chanting, "Earth bless the matriarch."

"What do you mean 'matriarch'?" Paxton asked. "Are you referring to Morgana Ravenwood?"

"First the innocent one, then the matriarch," Kay said. "There will be another, a betrayal of all."

A gust of wind blew through the trees and goosebumps arose on my arms.

"Kay," I said, reaching a hand forward to get him to look at me. "Will you start from the beginning?"

"Don't you see?" Kay said, his voice growing hoarse but his words tumbling out fast. "The book, she took the book from its rightful place and from it gathered secrets that weren't hers. She's wants what she shouldn't have, not after what she's done."

"Book?" I asked, glancing at Paxton. "What book?"

Kay closed his eyes. "Forgive me," he said, in a much more calm and sane voice. "The voices speak to me. It's hard to drown them out."

"You were talking about a book someone took from its rightful place," Paxton said, tapping his legs.

Kay raised his eyebrows and folded his hands in his lap. "You are trying to find who murdered that poor boy, Vyvan Woods, and now you're trying to find who desecrated Morgana's grave, yes?"

"Yes," Paxton and I said together.

"Both are missing hearts, with symbols written in blood around their bodies?"

"Yes," I said again.

"'Tis as I feared." Kay's eyes became unfocused, as if he were looking through a distant fog. "The Rite of Ascension is in play. I warned her, I warned her. If I had known what she had planned on committing, I would have barred her from my doors long ago. How did I not see the signs? How did I never warn the matriarch not to trust that girl?"

"Who?" Paxton asked, his tone clipped.

"She wants power," Kay continued. "But why she felt she needed to do it this way, I don't know. She was already a candidate."

"Kay, please," I said, my own impatience growing. I began rubbing my sweating hands on my knees. "We aren't understanding these riddles. What is going on?"

"No riddle, Dr. Grace." Kay finally looked up at me but his gaze was still clouded. "Our coven needs a new matriarch."

My mouth went dry. "What do you mean 'coven'? You don't mean a group of—"

"Witches?" Kay cackled, a hysterical note to it. "Of course! Who else could do these things? Who else knows of the Rite of Ascension?"

"What is the Rite of Ascension?" Paxton asked.

"It is cursed magic, meant to usurp power." Kay's face darkened again as he began chanting. "'Kill one of innocence, for their heart is pure. Violate one of power, for their heart is your spoor. Betray one of honor, for their pain your reign will ensure. Take their hearts and burn them all in one feat, for only then will your ascension to power be complete.'"

My arms erupted in goosebumps as Kay finished speaking. I glanced at Paxton to see he was a shade paler.

"I found her in my study," Kay said. "Anyone is allowed to seek knowledge from me or my library, but I startled her. Of course, I checked what she was researching." Tears spilled down Kay's cheeks. "Then she knew I knew and tried to kill me, but there she failed."

"So that's how your shoulder was injured?" I asked.

Kay nodded. "That and my own damned foolishness. It's why I'm here now."

"So is that why she was there?" Paxton asked. "To research the Rite of Ascension?"

"Yes, are you not listening?" Kay ran his hands through greasy hair, making it even more disheveled than before.

"How did she come to find this Rite of Ascension? Did she get it from a book? Uh, a scroll, tome?"

But Kay jerked back as if Paxton's words had been physical blows. "To have outsiders seeking our secrets." He muttered under his breath, his words once again becoming manic. "Is this to be my legacy? Can I tell them? Should I tell them? Can I, should I, can I?" Then he stopped. His voice became sane once again. "She found the knowledge in one of our oldest tomes. Our matriarch entrusted it to my care. How I failed her in the end."

Leaves crackled as I moved, I pulled one foot under me to make it easier to stand quickly. I asked, "Where is this tome now?"

Kay looked around the clearing, eyes lingering on something behind me before lifting his gaze to the heavens. "I have no idea. I ran away and fell down a steep cliff. My guess is that she assumed I died in the fall. I eventually made my way back to my residence, but I simply sealed it up so no one could get in. I didn't check to see if anything was missing." Kay heaved a quaking sigh. "There's no way to fix this now. I can't even go back to my home lest she find me and finish what she started."

"But you *can* fix it," I said, rising to my knees and placing a hand on Kay's right shoulder. "You can fix it all, Kay. Just tell us who's doing this."

"The rite demands three victims! You might still be able to save the last victim. She loves the last one and because of that, you might be able to stay her hand." Kay lunged forward and grabbed my arm, his grip like iron. "Our coven will be thrown into chaos without an heir to the matriarchy. You must protect our heirs at all costs!"

"We will," I said as I moved my foot up, to hold my balance. "If you just tell us who's in danger and who wants to hurt them."

"It's—" but several things happened at once.

A sharp buzz sounded past my ear and Paxton jumped up. I was splattered with something warm and wet. When I opened my eyes, Kay was slumped over, the tree behind him sprayed with blood and gore.

27

Holt

I scanned the woods, bouncing on the balls of my feet, hand on my holster. Officers and medics swarmed the entire forest. After we had called for backup, Lance brought in the whole cavalry. The entire forest was swarming with officers and medical professionals. Once Lance had seen we were both shaken but alright, he took our statements and took over the crime scene, insisting on removing us from the thick of things. He called for someone to bring Willow a change of clothes.

Over the bustle, I could still make out the sound of another UTV engine several officers had taken to find the sniper's position. I dug my feet in the ground to prevent myself from running after them, my back to a cluster of trees. Standing next to me was one of the medics, also facing away from the cluster of trees.

A twig snapped behind me, and I jerked around to see Willow in a matching blue CPD sweatsuit, two sizes too big for her. She was holding an evidence bag filled with her clothes in one hand. Blood smeared the inside of the plastic bag. As she stepped towards me, a damp, bloody towel swayed in her other hand.

The medic, a short but broad woman, took the bag and towel from Willow. "Is there anything else I can get for you, Dr. Grace?"

Willow shook her head and murmured a soft thanks. She tried to smile at the woman but her lips quivered.

I wrapped my arm around her shoulder and moved her to Gertha Mae's side, close to where Lance was standing. He looked around at us and his expression softened when he saw Willow.

"Our PD's colors suit you, Doctor."

Willow gave him a half smile just as her phone dinged. She pulled it from her sweatshirt pouch pocket and looked at the screen. When she angled it at me, I nodded after I read the message.

"Sheriff—" Willow's voice caught and she cleared her throat before starting again. "Before we had discovered Morgana's grave earlier, we were going to head back to Dr. Abernathy's place. He called to let us know that he had discovered something in his translation of Morgana's ledger. I got a text from him just now saying that he'd just finished translating it."

Lance frowned. "I don't think that's the best idea, especially after what you two just went through. Maybe it'd be best for you to stay here and allow—"

"Us to take Gertha Mae back to our car and let us get to Dr. Abernathy straight away." I finished his sentence at the look on Willow's face. Her face had paled at the mention of staying. "Glad we're on the same page. We'll call you with an update as soon as we have one."

Now in the car, zipping back up the winding roads that led to the Abernathy grounds, Willow stared out the windshield, motionless, eyes glassed over as we drove up the winding road to Dr. Abernathy's property. She held the Mylar blanket another medic had handed her before we left close around her shoulders, rubbing her free hand against her blue sweatpants.

I reached my hand across the console and squeezed Willow's thigh, a physical reminder that I was there. She didn't look at me but placed her hand over mine.

"I'll be okay, Paxton," she said quietly.

Are you sure? Do you need anything? I wish I could have spared you from that. I'll never let that happen to you again. I'm so sorry this happened.

Everything I wanted to tell her, to comfort her with, would either result in annoying or coddling her, neither of which she'd appreciate.

"Dr. Abernathy said that Horace would open the gate for us," Willow said. "I've let him know that we're on the way, but I've not gotten a reply."

I nodded, feeling her eyes on me as I didn't give a verbal response.

There was no way of knowing where the shot had been fired from. I had wanted to take off after the shooter, but seeing Kay sprawled against the tree and Willow pushing herself off the ground, covered in blood and brain matter...

We had come close to death in our cases together in the past. In other ways I had come close to losing her too. I had feared I would lose some part of her when she had to take a life for the first time, or if she had decided to stay at Conifer rather than work alongside me with the FBI. But we always came through. Her strength gave me strength. Her tenacity gave me hope. Her grace and kindness pushed me to be a better man.

The life I would lead if she were to die had flashed before my eyes today. The brokenness, the hollowness, the damned emptiness I would feel, had I'd lost the woman I loved again. It was selfish to be so caught up in how *I* would feel should something happen to her, but I didn't know any other way to process the implications. I couldn't lose her. I *wouldn't* lose her. I would do *anything* to make sure she was safe.

And I realized then that I did want to marry her. I wanted the two of us to be bound as closely together as two people could be. I loved her. I really, truly, deeply, wholly loved her.

"Paxton?"

I slowed the car and turned to face Willow, ready to ask her something just weeks ago I hadn't thought myself ready for.

"We're here," she said, "but the gate's already open."

Turning forward, I saw she was right. The iron gate had halted two thirds of the way through its track, just wide enough to let a car through.

"Think it's a fluke?" Willow asked.

"Must be." I pulled towards the goose-neck mounted call box and pressed the call button. "Horace? It's Agent Holt and Dr. Grace."

Silence.

After pressing the button a few more times and waiting a moment longer, I pulled the car forward and squeezed through the gate, nudging the iron open another inch. We stopped in the paved parking area in front of the house.

Willow and I got out and walked to the front door. She reached out to ring the bell before stopping and I saw it too: the door was ajar. Alarm grew in Willow's eyes when she looked back at me. Blood roared through my ears. I put myself in front of her.

Nothing else can happen to her.

I removed my service weapon from its holster for the second time that day. I did a press check and signaled for her to go sit in the car, to which she frowned but nodded.

I entered the house with painstaking steps, each one costing seconds. The front smelled of fresh air. The door had been left open for a while.

After pressing forward, sweeping my weapon left and right, I followed the darkened path to the library.

Splatters of dark liquid stained the wall, only a few drops. I rounded the corner of the long hallway, and the liquid turned into blotches. Hundreds of tiny streaks trickled down the wall.

Down the hallway, I found Horace lying face down on the carpet, the light from the windows casting his features in sharp contrast. A tea tray was scattered across the floor, the teapot and cup shattered into pieces in a pool of tea seeping into the rug. I stooped down to feel for a pulse.

Horace was still warm, but the murky sky outside reflected in his empty eyes. Fresh blood pooled beneath him.

"Shit."

I continued down the hallway, Glock pressed forward and entered the vacant library. The air was stale and tense, as if the house itself was holding its breath. Straight ahead, Dr. Abernathy's head rested on his desk along the back wall.

After clearing the room, I ran towards the doctor. My heart sank at the sight of him.

Blood drained from a hole in his left eye socket.

The doctor was dead.

28

Selena

Standing by the open front door, Selena watched the last of the police cars leave the property. She gripped the shawl the kind police officer had placed around her shoulders closer to her body, relishing in the warmth and softness of the garment. In her other hand she held a mug of hot tea, steam swirling in the air above the mug before dissipating into the cloudy sky.

It had taken some time to convince the police officer that she was alright. She knew she had looked a fright—her hair a mess from running her hands through it so often, her makeup smeared and streaky. But once the officer could see that the best thing she could do for Selena was to leave her in peace, she had gone, and Selena was free to breathe again.

She thought of the text messages she had sent as soon as she had been alone. She had gotten no other response than a thumbs up emoji. Her insides recoiled at the lack of communication. Sometimes she really hated modern technology.

Selena squinted at the bright white clouds above her. The coven would gather soon. Something as monstrous as the defilement of the matriarch's grave could not wait until the next summit. A fresh tear fell down her cheek and the wind evaporated it, causing the corners of her chafed eyes to sting.

To have watched her grandmother die was one thing. To see her decaying, mutilated corpse was something far worse. That even in death, where she should have been at peace, her matriarch was still not safe from the wiles of the power hungry.

Selena reentered the house and closed the front door behind her before leaning against it. Her head pressed against the wood, the sound of her hair rubbing between her skull and the door making goosebumps erupt on her skin. The clock on the side wall of the entryway chimed the hour.

They'd all be here at any moment.

Selena made herself walk into her grandmother's office. She started a fire and sat on one of the loveseat cushions, never taking her eyes from the flames even as people filed into the room. Soon a dozen figures were gathered around, none dressed in the ceremonial garb due to the urgency of Selena's summons. Once everyone had arrived, Celeste the last to walk through the door, a heavy silence weighed on the group.

A voice asked, "What's so urgent that it couldn't wait for the summit meeting tonight?"

Selena turned her gaze from the fire to those gathered before her. A fresh wave of tears ran down her face.

The whole circle stilled. Celeste assessed her with that same gentle, compassionate expression as she had at the committal service. But this time, there was a hint of unease.

And that unease pleased Selena.

"The matriarch's grave has been violated," she said, her voice steady despite the trails of tears on her cheeks.

Gasps and exclamations of horror resounded through the group.

"How can this be?" someone asked.

Selena stood. "Come and see."

She led them out the tall, glass screens, past the greenhouses, to her grandmother's empty grave. Footprints remained impressed in the dirt and moss. A line of forgotten police tape splayed over the head of the lion, now casting its mournful gaze at the sky. Black petals were strewn everywhere. Black Baccara petals, from the overturned beds in one of the greenhouses. The red symbols marred the lay stone.

Innocence. Violation. Betrayal.

A deep moan of grief and anger filled the air as the coven witnessed the desecration. Celeste fell to her knees at the edge of the grave.

"Why?"

"Who could have done this?"

"Is the earth against us?"

"Where is the Keeper of Knowledge when we need him?"

"My friends." Celeste's voice sounded over the panicky questions.

Everyone quieted. A twinge of unease sparked in Selena's chest as she watched Celeste rise from the ground and turn to face the coven.

"Panicking will solve nothing. Clearly something is at play here, and beyond our understanding. We need to retrace steps and think. As you all know, I saw the Vyvan boy's crime scene. Those symbols were around his body." She pointed to the lay stone. The group turned to squint at it, the light starting to dim as the afternoon faded.

"Surely the Keeper of Knowledge must have some information that can help us?" One of the group asked.

"It's no use," Selena said. "He vanished after my grandmother died, taking all his secrets and wisdom with him. His residence has been closed off. None can enter." She stopped, a tear falling down her cheek. "I've tried."

"Then what are we to do? The matriarch, the Keeper of Knowledge, and Vyvan have been taken from our midst. How are we to determine the next matriarch?"

"Yes, we need a matriarch to determine what we are to do!"

"Hush!" Selena said. "Let's not lose our heads. We know now that there is a traitor amongst us. A forbidden rite is being enacted and we must stop it before the final piece is finished. I suggest we all reconvene this evening for our summit. That way, all will be revealed and we can decide what we must do."

The group murmured their agreement and began their trek back to the house until only Celeste and Selena were left. They gazed at each other for a moment, each sizing up the other's resolve.

Finally, Celeste said, "I've kept the reporters away from this case. I doubt Morgana would have appreciated everything being publicized."

Selena nodded her thanks.

Celeste nodded in return. She looked down at the broken grave before she turned and left.

The unease from before came back in full force as Selena watched Celeste retreat. It wasn't for Morgana's peace that Celeste would call in a favor of that magnitude with the press. Despite her diplomacy, Selena knew who the real perpetrator was.

She had, after all, smelled the perfume.

29

Willow

It was only the middle of the afternoon, and it had already been such a long day.

I sat on the white couch in the middle of Dr. Abernathy's library, now facing his corpse. He lay face down at his desk, arms framing either side of his head. A bloody hole in his left eye still seeped blood, a perpendicular line of crimson dried to his skin.

Same as Kay.

I closed my eyes and tried to stop myself from shaking. So much death. I hated the intimacy of seeing a corpse, it was somehow more intimate than the presence of a lover. And yet despite resenting that intimacy, I wouldn't have been sorry to know the doctor better. The memory of our budding comradery caused my blood pressure to drop again. It had been a long time since I had to utilize my calming techniques, but I did so now, taking rattling breaths until I could release them smoothly.

A hand touched my shoulder and it was all I could do not to shriek.

"It's just me, honey." Paxton raised his other hand so I could see it and he lowered himself in front of me, never taking his gaze from my face. "You okay?"

I glanced over at Dr. Abernathy until Paxton grabbed my hands and squeezed, bringing my gaze back to him.

"You are the strongest, bravest women I know," he said. "But you don't have to be here. You have more than done your part. I can take you home and Lance and I can handle this."

Some part of me felt like I would usually be offended by the suggestion, but I couldn't summon the inclination.

"I want you to be here, but I care far more about your wellbeing than my desires." He squeezed my hands again. "Just say the word."

I took a breath so deep that my lungs visibly expanded through my oversized sweatshirt. After I released all the air from my lungs, I rolled my shoulders and managed a small smile at my partner.

"Thank you. Today's been a lot. But I want to see this through."

Paxton's eyes asked if I was sure, but he nodded. "Okay. Lance should be back any—"

The library door, half shut a moment before, burst open with enough force it bounced off its hinges.

"Four deaths in twenty-four hours!" Lance roared as he barreled into the room and started pacing back and forth. "And the grave of the town's most influential resident broken open and vandalized." He tugged at the ends of his hair, which stood on end from how often he'd run his fingers through it. "It's a wonder the reporters aren't calling for blood and my resignation."

Paxton stood. He glared at Lance after his noisy entrance made me jump.

Lance didn't notice Paxton's expression and began swearing badly enough to make the upholstery peel. "Why is it that I'm always cleaning up your messes?"

Paxton squared his shoulders. "That is uncalled for and you know it."

"Or massively effing convenient." Lance put his finger in Paxton's face.

Paxton swatted the sheriff's hand away. "What's that supposed to mean?"

"Hey!" I stood up and the two men stepped apart. "We're all stressed here but taking it out on each other is counterproductive."

Lance had the good sense to look a little ashamed. Once the anger in the room had dissipated somewhat, I said to the sheriff, "Take me through what we know one more time."

As I had hoped, Lance calmed at the prospect of a methodical approach.

"Based on how the hired help was found lying in the hallway," he said, "my guess is that he was on his way to give Dr. Abernathy his tea and was dead before he knew what was happening. I'd guess there was hardly any time between the tea tray crashing and the assailant entering the library to put a bullet into Dr. Abernathy's head."

Lance walked back to the library door and pointed down the hall. "Someone broke in through the gate and the front door, bypassing locks and keys."

He pointed towards Abernathy's desk. "The placement of the bullet in both the doctor and hired help indicates that this might not be the first time the perpetrator has killed someone."

Lance stood in the center of the door, holding his pointer finger out and thumb up in a finger gun as he took aim towards the desk. "The doctor had to have seen the killer straight on. I would hazard a guess that he heard the shot that killed his man, looked up, and then —" Lance imitated the sound of a gun firing. "It was too late."

I stood and walked over to the desk. "And any sign of the ledger and his translation notes are gone."

"Right in one." Lance huffed so hard, his mustache fluttered. "Remind me why the ledger was so important?"

"It was the clue connecting everything." Paxton stood still, aside from tapping his thumb against his holster. "Morgana gave it to Celeste, and Celeste brought it to us and we brought it to the doctor. Now we know that those symbols were directly connected to a forbidden bit of magic called the 'Rite of Ascension.'"

Lance nodded. "Right, I remember you saying so in your statements. So, was this it then? Is the rite complete?"

I shook my head. "It can't be. The MO is all wrong."

"Why do you say that?"

"I mean, the COD is different, there are no flowers, no symbols, we're *inside*."

"True, but how can we be sure what the MO really is?" Paxton said, with the tone he took when he was choosing to be the devil's advocate. "If Morgana was really the second victim, 'the one in power violated' or whatever the rhyme was, then she didn't die for the rite. Or, if she was killed, then it throws the rite's methodology off since she died weeks before Vyvan was murdered."

"But her grave site and corpse were clearly violated," I said.

Paxton rubbed his face. "Are we really talking about whether or not an heir to a coven of witches is on a murder spree to ensure her place as the next matriarch?"

I couldn't help but chuckle. "Yep."

"So why kill the doctor?" Lance asked. "Or the butler or Kay?"

"Kay never said who the killer was, but it was on the tip of his tongue," Paxton said.

I pointed at him. "We might be on the same page here. I think they all knew something. It would explain the different MO between these guys and the rite victims."

"Again, Morgana wasn't killed for the rite though."

"Maybe she didn't have to be," I countered. "Remember the verse Kay recited to us? 'Violate one of power, for their heart is your... something'. Gosh, I wish I could remember the words. Or better yet, have the damn book."

Lance stopped pacing. "We found a book. At Kay's crime scene."

"What kind of book?" Paxton asked.

"Old, leatherbound, held together by a clasp. It wasn't written in glyphs, but do you think—"

I cut him off. "Were there any other books there?"

"No, just the one. It was battered and covered in debris and was bloodstained."

"That has to be the tome Kay was talking about." I looked at Paxton, my heart rising in my chest. "He must have taken it with him when he ran from his cabin."

Paxton turned to Lance, who had taken out his phone and was tapping on the screen. "Bring it here, right away."

Lance clicked the screen and raised his phone up. "Already on it. While we're waiting for that, what else do we know?"

Still buzzing at the prospect of seeing the tome, it took me a second to organize my thoughts. I went back to Kay's final words.

She loves the last one. You must protect her!

"A woman's involved in this," Paxton said, as if he's been reading my thoughts. "But whether she's the one performing the rite, the one who'll be betrayed, or the one killing our informants, I don't know."

"If that's the case..." Lance paused, rubbing his mustache. "We might be looking at more than one perpetrator."

"Why do you say that?" I asked.

"A man could take on a male college student. With perseverance and brute strength, a man could break into and dig up Morgana's coffin. I'm not saying that there aren't women out there that could do it, but I know my town. Ain't no lady here who could do either of those things without help."

He had a point. The three of us fell back into silence. Still filled with energy, I couldn't bear to stand still so I scrutinized the untidy desk that was Dr. Abernathy's final resting place. There was something poetic, I supposed, about a scholar's death bed being his desk. Dr. Abernathy's desk was much like any academic's desk I'd ever met: untidy. The surface was covered in piles of loose bits of paper and dip pens. The antique desk lamp still illuminating the doctor's hair and face, throwing his eye socket into sharp contrast. I looked away from his face to the mess of papers underneath. They were all blank, aside from the drops of blood.

I took a step back, leaning on the window behind the doctor's desk, trying to get into his head. The dip pens and inkwells caught my eye again and I imagined the Doctor writing a letter or piece of literature, humming to himself while he sipped tea.

Without the ledger to guide us, we'd already exhausted all other clues. Lance had gone to check the Keeper's residence, a small cottage just outside of the Ravenwood property line, but, just as the Keeper had said, Lance couldn't get it no matter what or how hard he tried. Almost as if magic was keeping him out.

I looked up from the desk and asked, "Any word on Vyvan's autopsy?"

"No," Lance said. "Not yet."

I looked back at the desk, eyes falling on the back of Dr. Abernathy's legs. A fresh drip stain appeared at a very odd angle on the back of his gray pants. There was nothing on the desk that was leaking so I turned my head up at the ceiling but there was nothing directly above the desk. Then I noticed there was an odd distortion of the fabric around his thigh and the desk chair.

A bottle was jammed between his thigh and the cushion. "Hey, call Murphy back in here. I found something."

Paxton and Lance walked around the desk to see what I was looking at.

"You see that?" I pointed.

Lance stood and shouted, "Murphy, Sainz, get in here!"

A second later the pair entered. Lance directed Murphy to take pictures and Sainz to document what I had found. Lance pulled on a pair of latex gloves as the camera flashed, then knelt by the desk chair. He pulled the bottle out from the cushion. Light reflected off a clear liquid that covered his fingers.

He held the bottle to his nose. "Smells faintly acidic. Alcohol, maybe?" He rolled the bottle around. Engraved on the side in cursive letters was the word, *Ink.*

I let out an exhale. "I knew there was something about the desk that didn't make sense."

I looked at the desk again, noting the paper and dip pen only inches from his right hand, as if he had been holding it when he was shot and it slipped from his hand as he fell face first. I bent as close as I could to the pen and saw that there appeared to be no dried ink on the tip of the nib. Neither was there an inkwell anywhere on the desk. "The liquid coming from that bottle, it's clear right?" I pointed to paper underneath the doctor's hand and fallen pen. "What's the bet he wrote something here in invisible ink?"

30

Willow

"If you're right," Paxton said. "Then you should hold the page up to the light. Heat often triggers a chemical reaction in invisible ink to appear."

"What the hell." Lance threw up his arms. "Go for it. Dr. Grace, put on some gloves and see what happens."

Murphy handed me a pair of gloves and after I had slipped them on, Sainz handed me the paper. I walked around the desk to the lamp and held the page close to the light.

Within seconds, cursive ink appeared on the page, blooming into existence like flower petals unfurling. I read the letter aloud.

I am a paranoid old fool, I know, but it eases my mind to write this for my own records. I have finished deciphering the ledger for the FBI. They should be on their way now, though they are frightfully late. I hope all is well on their end. Regardless, the book they gave me proved indeed to be a ledger. Morgana, my dearest Morgana rest her soul, was meticulous to the nth degree. I shouldn't be surprised. She always was scrupulous, but in this case, her stringent record-keeping might solve this mystery.

The ledger describes everything. I already knew that she suffered from a rare heart disease, but I never knew that she had needed a transplant in order to live. She formed an agreement with an undesirable bunch to get the new heart to survive. In return, she allowed the traffickers to dispose of the donors' bodies on her property, away from the prying eyes of the police.

Clever woman! In her records, she referred to the dump site as the "Shipyard". This indicates that the "shipments" she mentions are all bodies. Gracious, there were so many bodies. And she knew the names of them all. At one point there were some ninety 'shipments' recorded being brought to the 'shipyard'. I don't know how she could have managed that.

She also gave the coordinates for the shipyard. Perhaps one day, I will venture out to see the place myself. I should be disgusted with her but I admit that I admire her ruthlessness. She was always—

The rest of the sentence was blotted, as if he had been startled before finishing.

Now he never would.

I looked up from the page and held it across the desk to Lance. He took it, once again exhaling hard enough to ruffle his mustache.

"Sounds like you were right about the trafficking connection," I said to Paxton. "I shouldn't have doubted you."

"Thanks, but in this case, finding out I'm right doesn't make me happy." Paxton finished writing something with a flourish in his notebook before snapping it shut and putting it in his pocket. "We should go check out those coordinates."

Lance's phone started ringing. He pulled it out of his pocket and answered. "Talk to me, Davis."

His phone was loud enough that I could hear the other side of the conversation.

"Hey boss. You wanted that book from the scene in the woods?"

"Yes, and I need it now. How close are you?"

"Well, sir..." Davis's voice grew uncomfortable. "We, uh, don't have it anymore."

Lance stilled and I looked at Paxton. "What do you mean, 'you don't have it anymore'?"

"We brought everything back to the clearing so that we could pack up and go. But that young woman? The one who was making a fuss at the crime scene? Well, she saw the book in one of the evidence bags and nearly flew out of her mind when she saw it. She asked me to let her keep it and wouldn't take no for an answer."

"You're telling me," Lance's voice lowered, a vein pulsing on his temple, "that you gave her a piece of evidence to an ongoing multi-homicide investigation?"

"No, sir!" Davis's voice became squeaky and he had to clear his throat. "No, never. When we threatened to charge her with obstruction, she finally backed off. But now we're back at the precinct and it's not here. That book is gone."

Eyes rolling into the back of his head, Lance pinched the bridge of his nose. "And where is Miss—"

My jacket pocket began vibrating. I pulled out my phone to read the caller ID but none was listed. I answered, a spike of anxiety dashing through me.

"Hello?"

"Hello, Dr. Grace? It's Celeste Black calling."

"Celeste?" My mind began reeling. I caught Paxton's eye and he bent close to the phone to hear the conversation. "Hi, what's up?"

Lance had hung up the phone and was looking at me. I mouthed, *It's Celeste.*

He stiffened. "Celeste?" He whispered. "But she—"

I waved him off to catch what Celeste was saying.

Lance pointed at the phone. "Put her on speaker."

"—hate to be a bother," she was saying. "But I think someone broke into my house."

"What? When? Are you okay?" I asked.

"I'm fine. It must have been recently. I was home, then ran an errand and came back. In that time someone let off a flower bomb in my kitchen. It's covered in petals."

Lance made a sudden movement closer to the phone. "Celeste, go to your car and stay put. Intruder could still be there. Why didn't you call me directly?"

"I did," she said, annoyed. "But it went straight to voicemail."

Lance pulled his phone from his pocket and cursed. "I was on the phone with Officer Davis... I'm sorry. Are you alright?"

"I'm fine, Terran, don't mother me."

"We'll send someone your way—"

"Actually, Agent Holt." Celeste cut him off, an edge coming to her tone. "I'd really appreciate if you guys would come here. Something's off. There's... I think it's a black dahlia? It's on my counter and I don't know where it came from. Maybe it's nothing, but after seeing the lilies—"

"Stay there, we're on our way," Lance said, darting out the door without waiting for an answer.

We left Murphy to stand guard and ran after Lance, Sainz trailing behind us. By the time we reached the courtyard, Lance was giving instructions to the limited officers on scene. Everyone's face was a mask of grim determination.

"Get the crime scenes in there secure," Lance called out. "ME should be on their way shortly."

"Where are you going, Sheriff?" One of the officers asked.

"To hunt down a lead," Sainz said. He nodded to Lance. "Go, Sheriff. We'll handle it from here."

Lance gave him a single nod and sprinted to his car. "I'll see you two there," he called to us over his shoulder.

The tiny crowd of officers parted for us as we made our way to our own car. After we both got in, Paxton chased after Lance who was already a quarter of a mile ahead of us.

"There's no way they aren't, at the very least, hooking up," Paxton said.

I gave him a side eye before turning my gaze back out the front window. I rested my elbow on the window ledge and rubbed my forehead. "Something's wrong, Paxton."

"What part of this whole mess *isn't* wrong?"

"No, I mean..." I chewed my bottom lip. "Remember how Kay was saying that the person who tried to kill him, who looked up forbidden information? He said that she was already a candidate for the matriarchy for the local coven."

Paxton nodded. "Yeah."

"From everything we've pieced together, there are only two people that could be," I said. "Selena and Celeste."

Paxton nodded again. "Yes, I came to the same conclusion."

"Why would Selena desecrate her grandmother's grave?"

"Why would Celeste desecrate her mentor's grave?"

I conceded his point. "It doesn't make sense for either of them to go forward with this. What's the point?"

"Jealousy? If there really *is* a coven that really *is* in need of a new matriarch and both Selena and Celeste are candidates, that can't be pretty." Paxton hit his thumbs against the steering wheel. "The granddaughter versus the protégé? Kinda messed up."

"You're taking the idea of this being a political battle between witches really well," I commented, a half smile growing on my lips.

Paxton shrugged. "We know the organ trafficking ring is connected now. But until we get more solid evidence in that direction, this is the best lead."

Which was fair.

It took us about half an hour of winding through the forest and single lane back roads to get to Celeste's house on the other side of town. By the time we pulled in front of the small white cottage covered in vines, Lance was already out of his car and peering into Celeste's gray Audi.

He looked at us and shook his head.

"Don't know why he expected her to listen to him," Paxton muttered.

The three of us met on the small driveway and I pointed at the front door. It was open, swinging back and forth from the slight breeze. A wind chime in front of the door jangled.

I waited by the car as the two men pulled out their guns and held them at the low ready as they walked towards the house.

"Conifer PD," Lance called out as he pushed on the door. "Celeste? We're coming in."

They walked inside. I tapped my fingernails against my teeth, rocking as I waited.

If Celeste was the candidate for the matriarchy, why was she being targeted as the next victim? Unless this was a hoax? But if it was, why the subterfuge? She hadn't been at the Ravenwood Estate to take the tome. Unless... she did say she had to run an errand before coming back to her house. Was that it?

But Selena had been on the Ravenwood Estate all day. The nagging feeling of having missed something about Selena came back to me. I walked over to Celeste's car and looked inside before opening the driver's door. As soon as I did, a light, airy perfume hit my nose.

That was it.

Celeste's perfume was never at the first crime scene. Not until after her unexpected arrival.

Paxton popped his head back out the door and beckoned me to come in.

Celeste's house opened into a narrow hallway. The walls lingered with the scent of her perfume mixed with something floral and tinged with something metallic.

Lance's footsteps sounded from the hallway to the right. Doors creaked open, rustling coming from within.

Paxton led the way forward into a small kitchen combined with the dining and living rooms. A sliding glass door opened into Celeste's backyard. Dark petals were strewn all over the floor, like a bomb of flowers had gone off in this one space.

A single black dahlia lay on the kitchen counter. Next to it, still wet, was a single drawing of the third symbol from the pattern, drawn in a dark red substance.

Betrayal.

31

Selena

Selena thought about the time she first learned of the dead's presence here, on the Ravenwood Estate, mere weeks ago. She'd known her grandmother had been hiding something. What leader didn't have something to hide? What matriarch didn't have secrets? Selena could admit to prying. She had snooped through her grandmother's office, rifled through her desk, pawed at every nook and cranny of her manor home for the secret passages that all old houses possess.

But her grandmother had either been aware of Selena's meddling or had simply been too cunning. She had never found anything, although she had gotten close to uncovering some of her grandmother's secrets once, only a short while ago. She'd overheard her grandmother's phone conversation. And she'd discovered her grandmother's rapid heart failure.

The reason her grandmother had formed an alliance with the organ traffickers.

One day, Selena stood, staring at the forbidden gate. Once again, there had been fresh tire tracks through the mud on the other side. Why wasn't she allowed to know this secret?

Perhaps Celeste had already known this one too. She had gotten to see the Forbidden book. Why not this too? Her chest had tightened at the thought. How could her grandmother have done this to her?

Selena had taken a deep breath, and expanded her thoughts into the ether, just as her grandmother had taught her. And though she had tried this countless times in the past to catch a glimpse of the secrets hidden behind the gate, this time was different.

Dozens of voices suspended in the ether called out, whispering her name.

The voices of the dead were calling to her.

She'd obeyed. She'd listened to their summons.

With their guidance, she had opened the impenetrable gate and followed the path on the other side. The voices led her deep into the woods to discover her grandmother's biggest secret.

There were so many bodies.

Dismembered, dismantled, discarded. Remains scattered and littered across the forest floor. The stench of dozens of decaying, rotting corpses was enough to have her collapsing to her knees and heaving her stomach's contents out so hard, she had thought she'd vomit her stomach up too.

She had rolled onto her back, the taste and smell of bile burning the back of her throat.

This was worse than she could ever have imagined. Yet... Selena knew the secret now.

She'd sat up, holding her hand to her face to ward off the smell. Expanding her thoughts out into the ether, she'd listened to the voices again. They told her what she should do.

So she had run all the long miles back to the estate, determined to have it out, finally, with her matriarch.

Selena had raced into the house, burst through her grandmother's office door, to see a tall man clutching her grandmother's shoulders and shaking her. In the half-speed of a nightmare, the man released her grandmother with a startled push away from him. The older woman lost her footing, tumbling back into the side table by the love seat.

A water pitcher tipped off the wobbling table and shattered, sending shards of etched glass and water across the floor. Morgana slipped on the water and glass, hitting the back of her head on the sharp corner of the stone hearth. She slumped and stilled with an awful finality.

"Grandmother!" Selena rushed into the room, passed the man as he pulled something from his hip, and dropped to her knees next to body.

She put her fingers to her grandmother's neck, her ear to the woman's lips but there was no sign of life. As she looked back up at her grandmother's face, her blood, thinning as it mixed with the spilled water, already beginning to pool under her long, gray hair.

No kind nor amount of magic could revive her now.

Selena turned towards the man who was re-holstering his handgun, still standing in the middle of the room. The first thing she noticed was how handsome he was, with a tall muscular figure clad in a white button up, black slacks, and suspenders. A strand of flaxen hair had fallen from the bun tied at the nape of his neck. The second thing she noticed was that, as he massaged the palm of his hand with the thumb of his other, he was missing the index finger of his left hand.

"Who are you?" Selena asked, standing.

The man cocked an eyebrow. "I was about to blow your head off and you ask who *I* am?"

"You had the good sense not to, so who are you?"

The man scoffed. "I could ask the same, aside from being the late Madame Ravenwood's granddaughter."

This time Selena raised her eyebrows. "I guess now you could say that I..." She looked once more at her grandmother's wide, sightless eyes before turning her back on the corpse completely and facing the nine-fingered man head on. "Am Lady Ravenwood."

"Please to meet you, my lady," The man said, an ironic grin forming on his lips. "Now, perhaps you will be more reasonable than your grandmother proved to be."

"And how might that be, sir?"

He eyed her, an annoying smirk pulling across his jawline. "You truly don't know who I am, or why I am here?"

"Clearly you had a grievance with my grandmother, though as to who you are or why, I can only guess." Selena folded her arms across her rib cage, purposefully drawing attention to her upper assets. "My grandmother didn't have many enemies. None, actually."

The man gave the smallest glance to her chest before saying. "The only reason your grandmother was still alive was because of us. Without us, her heart would have given out long ago."

Selena narrowed her eyes at him. "What are you talking about?"

"Let's just say she didn't have to go through the regular channels to receive a heart transplant."

Selena's mind raced. Her grandmother's heart failure, the mass grave of bodies in the woods. She recalled her grandmother's relief after the news broke last week that the organ trafficking ring had been broken up. And then the fear she'd had after a call the previous night. This man must be connected to the traffickers somehow.

"So, what," Selena said. "You came here to collect her debt?"

The man quirked his brow as if Selena's guess was close but not quite on the money. "She fulfilled her contract with us."

Selena huffed, nearly growling at the man. She raised her voice when she asked, "Then what did you want?"

"It doesn't matter anymore. I—" He had put his hand on his gun again, turning his head to the side, as if listening to something.

Selena heard nothing. Not a bird chirping. Nor the wind howling.

The man had a small piece in his ear. A wire connecting him with someone from the outside. He wasn't the one in charge.

Which meant that she still could come out on top if she played her cards right.

"What were the stipulations of your contract with my grandmother?" she asked.

He glanced at her before looking again to the side. After giving a very small dip of his head, he turned to her fully. "We'd get her a new heart any time she needed one and in return, we could use the grounds of the Ravenwood Estate as the... final resting place for the generous donors."

Selena held the man's gaze for a whole minute.

After everything her grandmother held dear, all the community service, helping those in need, the charity, the *blatant* philanthropy, this? To have, all along, been assisting an organ trafficking ring and profiting off it as well? Oh, the scandal. How far had her grandmother fallen.

Selena smiled, a new idea taking shape.

"Let me guess, you were going to offer her a new heart in exchange for using the land indefinitely and she refused?"

The corners of the man's lips lifted. "Precisely. She'd wanted to be out from under our thumb for quite some time, but the fear of being outed had too tight a grasp on her. We all like reassurance that our secrets won't be revealed." His amused expression vanished and eyes like a rabid predator bored into her own. "Don't we, Lady Ravenwood?"

Selena snorted. "Please, spare me." She walked over to the man and patted his chest, admiring the firmness of his pectorals. "Your secret is safe with me."

The man watched her as she walked over to the shattered water pitcher. "You don't—"

"I don't care if you continue to use the grounds," she told him. "I don't care that my grandmother has been lying to the good people of

Conifer for years. I don't even care that she's betrayed her coven, although that one stings a teensy bit, I'll admit."

She faced the man. "All I care about is taking my rightful place as the coven's matriarch. With your organization's support, I would be unstoppable."

The man narrowed his eyes at her. "And why should we help you?"

"Because I'll be a canary in a heartbeat, pun intended. I know exactly where the shipyard is and now, thanks to you, I know the details of your arrangement with Morgana. You could kill me, right here and now, sure, but I am much more valuable to you alive. Who do you think they'll believe if the granddaughter of the beloved philanthropist revealed that she had been coerced into assisting the trafficking ring before it had been dismantled?"

"And who do you think they'll believe when your grandmother's medical records are leaked to the public?" the man asked. "We can just let that tidbit slip before abandoning this estate forever, taking all incriminating evidence with us. We don't need you."

"Assuming that I haven't been recording you this whole time, ready to turn this whole conversation over to the police." Selena pointed around the room. "Grandmother did like to feel safe, as you pointed out."

The man glared around the room before facing her again, clearly trying to decide whether to call her bluff. As he was about to answer, he tilted his head to the side again.

After a moment, he nodded. "Very well. We have a deal."

She smirked at him again, pulling down her shirt to real a little more of her cleavage. "Excellent. Now do tell me, what was your name?"

"I'm the Liaison," he said, returning the expression. "That's all you need know."

∼

Selena had never been afraid of blackmail.

It was clear she was the best choice for the next matriarch, despite her grandmother's proclivities otherwise. Who cared that Celeste had shown a rare talent at an age younger than witch powers typically emerged? What about Selena? That woman didn't, *couldn't*, understand the power Selena now possessed, nor that it was about to multiply tenfold with the completion of the rite. Her grandmother had relied on the instruments of mortals. Selena relied on the wiles of the ether.

What a slap in the face Celeste's very presence had been. How much more so when Celeste was taught the same secrets as Selena. If her grandmother had thought friendly rivalry would bring the two young witches closer together, she had been wrong. When Celeste had beaten Selena in that race in their adolescence, her grandmother shared Selena's birthright with her rival. And Celeste had done nothing. As if to rub that victory in Selena's face. Selena's heart was forever pitted against her.

Selena would not bow to the whims of others any longer. She would not be imprisoned by her own foolishness. She would not let anyone take anything from her. Not now, not ever.

Selena took a deep breath, her eyes closed, as she wiggled her toes into the earth beneath her feet. It was frigid, yes, but the crisp, sharp air, the cold dirt, the rustling of the forest around her made her come alive. Reaching her mind out into the ethers again, Selena sensed the pull into the earth, the voices of the dead calling out to her once more.

She heard them.

That was her payment. Their presence here was what afforded her this chance, after all. Without them, her plan could never have come this far. With them, everything was nearly within her grasp.

It was almost pathetic how selfish her grandmother had turned out to be. Yet, it might have been the last gift that old woman ever gave to Selena—the means of securing her reign as the rightful next matriarch.

And so, at finding her grandmother dead and the Liaison to the trafficking ring in her, Selena's house, she'd concocted a plan.

She had paid a visit to the Keeper of Knowledge's Library. Hidden in the Keeper's personal library shelves, she had found the forbidden book. She'd greedily read the pages, searching to find the perfect means to enable and ensure her take-over. And that was when she had found the entry to the Rite of Ascension.

But as she'd copied out the instructions, the Keeper had found her. Panicked, she'd fled, but not until after she'd left had she remembered that she hadn't hidden the book.

So, the Keeper of Knowledge had to die.

The Liaison had been more helpful than she'd anticipated in that regard. She'd needed someone to do the dirty work of silencing witnesses. She'd watched the police gear up to go into the woods after they'd discovered what she'd done to her grandmother's grave. When she'd asked why, the police officer explained that they had found something at the grave that might give them a clue pointing to the culprit.

A suspicion had darkened her mind, so she'd sent Liaison to tag along after them. When he'd called to tell her the Keeper of Knowledge was dead and that he was now following the FBI agent and his little consultant to the Abernathy estate, Selena feared that all was lost. When she'd discovered that the police had the forbidden tome, it had taken everything in her to keep her rage in check. It had taken every ounce of her powers and finesse to take it back, but she'd done it. She had the Forbidden Tome and her grandmother's ledger.

And the Liaison had pulled through, too. He'd silenced all witnesses and kept the police off her trail. But most importantly of all, he'd been the one to teach her how to extract the organs the rite demanded.

After his jaunt on the Abernathy grounds, Liaison had brought Celeste to Selena, having gone to her house and knocked her unconscious before bringing her to the Ravenwood Estate. He'd followed her instructions of setting the stage of Celeste's kidnapping with the petals and the single, black dahlia. He understood the necessity of symbolism being honored. He'd even brought her grandmother's ledger and the translation done by her ex-lover. With those two items and the forbidden tome, she'd have everything she'd need to condemn Celeste.

Now, Celeste was tied with her front to a sturdy tree. her arms wrapped around the tall trunk. Despite the ropes holding her in place, her heavenly radiance was not diminished. The wind pulled at the tendrils of her obsidian hair and plucked at the sheer gown adorning her petite, pale frame.

Before she and Liaison had tied her to the pyre, Selena had changed Celeste out of her clothes and into the white chemise with all the delicacy of a mother. Celeste, still knocked out cold, hadn't fought back. She looked just like a witch about to be burned.

Selena could admit that an iota of guilt pooled in her soul as she looked at Celeste. Her rival yet her coven sister. If she could go back and change the past, she'd do it to prevent this story from unfolding.

But that fleck of guilt in Selena was not strong enough to stop the rite. She would be her grandmother's sole heir. She would be the next matriarch. None could stop her, not once she laid out all the evidence to the coven at the summit that night.

She conjured a table and placed the two ornamental boxes on top, one containing Vyvan's heart and the other containing the half-decayed remains of her grandmother's. Then she pulled out the knife she had used to carve those vessels from their hosts and placed it on the table.

Celeste stirred, rolling her shoulders. Selena kept her eyes on the woman's spine.

Betray one of honor, for their pain your reign will ensure.

32

Celeste

A monotonous throbbing brought Celeste back from the far-off wiles of the ether. With each beat of her heart, pain thumped through her head so intense that she wished she could fall back into oblivion. The pain didn't exist there.

But she was cold. A breeze caressed her bare arms, pulling at the light fabric encasing her and making it impossible for her to find comfort in the blackness of moments before.

Where was she?

Celeste peeled her eyes open, but they were met with dim, spinning images. Dizziness threatened to wrench her stomach, so she closed them again. How had opening her eyes taken so much energy? She leaned forward and rested her head on something hard and upright in front of her.

Which made her pause and reassess her body.

She was standing, her head resting against the same thing that her arms were wrapped around. Almost as if she was giving a tree a hug. The hard thing in front of her smelled wet and woody. Then something floral caught at her nose and she remembered.

Flowers.

The flowers.

There had been flowers, everywhere.

Celeste had come home from Ravenwood Estate, heart heavy. The emergency meeting that Selena had called was just another blow to the coven. Celeste had hated seeing the looks of shock and horror on the others' faces. But to see Selena, austere and rigid Selena, reduced to a messy, blubbering version of herself had been yet another red flag in a long line of them.

Selena had always been haughty and aloof. She had shown nearly no emotion when relaying the news of her grandmother's death and even less on the day of her funeral and committal. But Morgana's grave being broken into? That's what had set Selena over the edge? Something about the way she had said 'all will be revealed tonight' with that cold glean over her mascara-streaked cheeks had sent fingers of disquiet down Celeste's spine.

Selena was performing a rite under their noses. Celeste recognized the signs now, the missing heart, the glyphs, the flowers. She'd read about them, all those years ago in Morgana's study when her mistress had allowed her to read the Forbidden Book. If only she could remember which rite it was. That would lead them, the coven and police alike, to the perpetrator.

Celeste wished that she could talk to someone, someone she trusted, about everything that had happened. Terran came unbidden to her mind, an image of him gazing at her with those gorgeous blue eyes. Would he ever come around? Finally address the giant elephant in the room? She'd already hinted at her feelings for him. How much more straightforward did he expect her to get?

Sighing, Celeste opened her front door. She walked down the short hall to her kitchen, planning on placing her bag on the counter as she always did. But she stopped short when she saw the dark flower petals littering her kitchen, as if someone had thrown them about like confetti.

The tap of unease she had felt all day began dripping again. She bent, purse strap falling from her shoulder to her arm, and picked up one of the petals. Rubbing it between her fingers, she held the petal to her nose and inhaled the sickly-sweet smell.

She let her purse fall to the floor as she stood up. Taking deep breaths, she scanned around the open room. The coffee table was tidy, with only a couple magazines on top. Every book was in order on her shelves. She even squinted at the lock on the back door to ensure it was locked. It was. She turned back to her kitchen.

Then she saw it.

A single black dahlia lay on the counter. Those were cursed flowers, the flowers of betrayal.

"Earth below and stars above," Celeste whispered.

Hands beginning to shake, she pulled her phone out of her pocket and called Terran. The call went straight to voice mail. A cold sweat broke out on her forehead so she dialed Dr. Grace. The doctor picked up on the second ring.

"Hello?"

"Hello, Dr. Grace? It's Celeste Black calling."

"Celeste?" A rustling came through the phone. "Hi, what's up?"

"Hi," Celeste said, trying to keep her voice steady. "Um, so, listen. I really do hate to be a bother, but I think someone broke into my house."

"What?" Willow's voice was startled. "When? Are you okay?"

"I'm fine. It must have been recently. I was home, ran an errand, came back and in that time someone let off a flower bomb in my kitchen. It's covered in petals." Celeste winced at how stupid it sounded once she said it aloud.

"Celeste, go to your car and stay there." Terran's voice came over the line. "Intruder could still be there. Why didn't you call me directly?"

Relief and disappointment washed through Celeste at the sound of his voice. "I did but it went straight to voicemail."

A pause followed by a curse. "I was on the phone with Officer Davis. I'm sorry. Are you alright?"

"I'm fine, Terran, don't mother me."

Another rustling sound and Agent Holt said, "We'll send someone your way—"

"Actually, Agent Holt, I'd really appreciate if you guys would come here. Something's off. There's... I think it's a black dahlia?" Celeste picked up the flower on the counter, twirling it in her fingers. "It's on my counter and I don't know where it came from. Maybe it's nothing, but after seeing the lilies—"

"Stay there, we're on our way," Terran said and she could hear heavy footsteps going away from the phone.

"Hang tight and wait outside," Agent Holt said. "We'll be there soon."

"Okay," Celeste said and hung up the phone. She took a deep breath and set the flower back on the counter. Bending to grab her purse from the floor, she froze.

It wasn't there anymore.

Celeste looked around, eyes darting everywhere until they landed on a pair of shoes standing in the hallway. A man stepped out of the shadows. She shrieked, the sight of the golden-haired giant stepping towards her sending her heart into a panicked sprint. Darting back, she stepped behind her kitchen island to put something between her and the man.

"Who do you think you are?" Celeste demanded, anger now replacing her panic. She raised herself to her full height of five-foot-one. "Get out of my house."

The man chuckled and seemed to grow taller as he stepped closer to the island. A gun was holstered at his waist. "Gladly," he said, spreading his hands out in front of him. One of his fingers was missing. "Won't you come with me?"

"You had your warning." Swelling with power, Celeste raised her hand as a conduit for her spell before the man pulled the gun from his holster. Before she could react, he reached across the island and knocked her on the head so hard she saw stars before her world had tipped into blackness.

Darkness.

Oblivion.

The ether whispered in her ear.

No, that was the sound of leaves rustling around her. She came to her body once more, her forehead still resting on something upright in front of her. The breeze whooshed by, chilling her.

Breeze? Why was she outside?

She was standing on something dry and uneven. Becoming aware of hundreds of sharp pricks into her feet, ankles and legs, she tried to adjust her step, but the pricks were unceasing.

Then Celeste heard something so deep, she could feel it in her chest. Drums. The deep beat struck every other heartbeat. Over the drums, she heard a voice. A voice she knew, shouting. But she couldn't make out the words. They mixed together, as if put into a blender before reaching her ears, turning the words into alphabet soup in her mind.

The voice was buttery smooth, a woman's. The tone was strident, growing in anger and intensity. Then the breeze carried the scent of a perfume, heavy and hazy, to Celeste's nose.

Selena. Selena was nearby.

Celeste inhaled through her nose and opened her eyes again. Her surroundings started to come into focus, though barely. A tall figure with long dark hair stood in front of her, arm outstretched towards her. Celeste tried to grab the hand pointing at her but, for some reason, she couldn't move. The figure came into sharper focus and Celeste watched Selena's hair whip from side to side as she gestured towards Celeste.

Celeste blinked hard and looked around. Beside Selena was a table filled with multiple items Celeste didn't recognize. Glinting in the light of the lit torch propped in an iron holder were two boxes.

Next to them were two books. Behind the boxes was a wicked knife. Selena's knife. The pricks in her feet started stinging and she looked down to see that she was surrounded by bundles of hay and sticks.

Movement in front of her brought Celeste's gaze to a crowd of people standing in front of both her and Selena. The crowd's eyes were trained on Selena but a few people cast furtive looks towards Celeste.

"It is due to her that our coven has mourned so much in recent weeks." Selena's words finally penetrated Celeste's thick skull. "Who had access to that innocent boy, Vyvan? She did. Who stood to gain from my grandmother's untimely death? She did. Who went behind our backs and gave this—" Here Selena held something up. Celeste couldn't make it out until light reflected off the clasp of the notebook. Morgana's ledger. "—a notebook detailing secrets of our matriarch to the police? She did."

"Did you actually see her give that to the police?" someone shouted.

Selena lowered her head. "We all have our ways of knowing things."

"She wasn't the only one who stood to gain from your grandmother's death," another voice called out. "You had something to gain too, didn't you Selena?"

Selena started pacing in front of Celeste, the movement bringing the dizziness back to Celeste's head. She choked down the nausea starting to rise in her throat.

Selena's voice dipped to almost a whisper. "I know beyond a shadow of a doubt that Celeste has sought forbidden magic, to the point of assaulting and killing Kay, our Keeper of Knowledge."

Silence emanated.

"That is quite the accusation," another in the crowd said. "Do you have proof?"

"His body was found in the woods of Ravenwood Estate earlier this very day. He was hiding out in fear of further injury. Found in his possessions was the tome of forbidden knowledge." Selena stopped in front of the table and ran her fingers along the spine of one of the books. "Our dear Celeste has performed one of the rites from these pages. See here the hearts of Vyvan and our own, felled matriarch." Selena's voice trembled as she pointed to the boxes on the table. "I was to be the next and last of her victims. After every one of you left this afternoon, Celeste cornered and attacked me. By a miracle, I was able to overtake and bind her. Now is the time for her to pay for her crimes!"

A murmur swept through the crowd and Celeste's head spun more than it had a moment ago. Selena must have finally cracked under all the pressure she had been under since her grandmother died.

"No." Celeste's voice was slurred. "Not true."

"See here?" Selena screamed. "How she tries to deny the truth with the evidence that I have laid before you?"

Wait, since when had Kay died? Why hadn't she said anything about that before now? Celeste opened her mouth to ask this but Selena continued.

"Her crimes deserve death. Let us set her alight like those heathens before us!"

The crowd murmured again.

"Selena, this is not our way," someone said. "You know better than anyone that we have laws in place. She is to stand trial."

"To be accused of such a heinous act removes her from the matriarch candidacy." Selena's eyes had grown wide and bloodshot. "That leaves me to make these choices, for our own protection."

"You cannot take the law into your own hands!"

Selena screamed in rage again. "Fool! She shall burn!" She grabbed the torch from its stand and ran towards Celeste. Several members of the crowd rushed forward but Selena threw the torch at the hay and sticks encircling Celeste.

Flames began licking Celeste's feet.

33

Willow

"This has to be the way to the Shipyard." Lance pointed towards the metal gate.

My eyes traced the metal bars of the gate. It was a miniature replica of the Ravenwood Estate's back entrance. The third symbol was framed in the top portion of the barrier, seeming to beckon us forward.

We were standing at a crossroads in the woods of the Ravenwood Estate. Once we had realized that she was the final victim to the rite, Lance, Paxton, and I all barreled our way from Celeste's house to the Ravenwood Estate. Lance had called all his team and backup to meet us there.

We had been canvassing the woods for over half an hour, steadily losing daylight. Half the team had followed the path in the woods not far from Morgana's grave. The other half had gone around the back of the property and was following the road past the back gate. Paxton and I, once again decked out in field gear though this time with flashlights, were standing with Lance. He also wore a Kevlar vest. One of his hands rested on his holster as he continued pointing at the metal gate.

"I'm going to make an educated guess and say that the back road and this pathway lead to the same place," Lance said.

Paxton nodded. "Makes sense. Send some guys down that direction and we'll keep walking up that path here—"

"Sir!"

A little ways up the path, Sainz and Murphy waved at us. Paxton and I followed Lance over to where the two were standing. Sainz gestured behind him. "Look what we found, Sheriff."

Down a small incline was a black Porsche, nestled in the trees. Behind the tires were two small indented lines in the leaves, curving through the trees and out of sight.

Paxton and Lance jogged down to it. Lance peaked through the windows while Paxton rounded the back.

"No license plate," he called up to us.

Lance's voice was tight. "Celeste's head scarf is in the backseat." He stepped from the driver's window to put his hand over the hood. "It's still warm. So recently driven."

"But who drove it out here?" I asked. "Selena?"

Sainz raised a shoulder as Paxton and Lance came jogging back.

Lance's pale face stood out against the darkening forest backdrop. "She's got to be close."

"Uh, sir?" Murphy had taken a few steps away from the group. He turned back to us. "Do you hear that?"

We all grew quiet. Wind blew through the trees, rustling the foliage. A few of the officers shifted their weight, causing a soft susurrus of fabric. And there it was, faintly, in the distance.

The steady beat of a deep drum.

Murphy caught my eye. "Drums are never a good sign," he whispered.

Sainz rolled his eyes. "This is ain't some dumb movie, Murph."

"But in this case, he probably has a point." Lance pointed at the pair. "You two, head up the path here and see where it goes. Everyone else, follow me."

Lance led the way down the trail. Sainz and Murphy headed back to the gate while everyone started spreading out behind Lance, stray leaves crunching under our feet. The fading daylight was getting harder to see the deeper into the forest we traversed. The leaves and branches were turning into a canvas overhead, as if cocooning us in.

Paxton fell into step beside me. "If anything goes down, I want you to run."

I furrowed my brow at him. "And leave you? No way."

"We're dealing with a demented killer performing a murder rite," Paxton said. "Willow, I can't lose—"

"Hold it." Lance held his arm out and we all stopped. He held his finger to his mouth before pointing. Everyone moved to stand behind a tree.

Straight ahead was a large clearing. Several large lanterns were hanging throughout the area, lighting the space up with dim, flickering light. Branches and leaves were so tightly woven above that it made a kind of ceiling over the area. The ground was bare, even of grass and leaves.

A crowd of people all stood facing away from us. Every single one of them were dressed in a white robe, putting in mind an army of ghosts standing at attention.

From behind his own tree, Lance gestured for us all to branch out. I stayed put as the other officers started moving, working on surrounding the clearing. I caught Paxton's eyes as he crouched behind the next tree.

Stay there. Be safe. He mouthed at me.

On the far end of the clearing, a female voice was calling out over the crowd. A female voice that I recognized.

Selena.

I followed the sound of her voice and spotted her pacing back and forth in front of the crowd. Behind Selena was a tall stake. A small figure was hugging the tree, as if protecting it from harm.

I looked around and saw that I was alone. All the officers had dispersed around the clearing. Careful to stay out of sight, I began inching my way around the clearing, all the while keeping Selena in my sights.

"—such a heinous act removes her from the matriarch candidacy." Selena's eyes were wide and bloodshot, nothing at all like the mourning woman I had met earlier that day. "That leaves me to make these choices, for our own protection."

She gestured to the trunk and I followed her movement.

An icy chill erupted down my whole body, freezing me in place. Now that I was closer, I could make out the small figure hugging the trunk better. It was Celeste, tied front against a tall stake. She was slumped against the pyre, the ropes around her holding her body upright. Surrounding her feet and legs were bundles of hay and sticks.

"You cannot take the law into your own hands!" someone in the crowd shouted.

Selena screamed, sparks seeming to fly from her eyes. "Fool! She shall burn!" She whirled around and from a table covered in books and boxes behind her, she grabbed a lone torch from its stand. The crowd rushed forward but Selena threw the torch at the hay and sticks encircling Celeste.

The hay immediately caught fire.

Pandemonium ensued as the officers ran from the trees and into the clearing. The crowd began running in every direction. Several people ran towards Selena, grabbing her as she tried to duck between them to get away. Her screams were the loudest noise in the din.

I watched from the trees, expecting more people to run to Celeste's aid, but only Lance had run towards her. He was frantically kicking the smoking hay away, while also cutting through the bindings securing Celeste to the tree. Taking a deep breath, I leapt from my hiding spot and sprinted as fast as I could to the pyre. I skidded to a stop by the base of the stake and started coughing as the smoke billowed up. I grabbed the knife from Lance, and after kicking the rest of the smoldering bundles of hay aside, began sawing at the rope around the stake.

Celeste groaned, head and eyes rolling. Lance stood behind her, holding her weight against his chest as the ropes began loosening.

"It's okay baby, we've almost got you free. Just hang on."

Eyes stinging, throat burning, I cut through the last of the rope. Celeste slumped back and Lance caught her. Lifting her in a fireman's carry, Lance stepped back, coughing. The edge of Celeste's white smock was smoldering so I started smothering it as I moved with Lance away from the pyre to the edge of the clearing.

He laid her down and I dropped to my knees beside her.

"Go, I got her!" I shouted.

Lance gripped Celeste's hand. "Don't you die on me, Celeste, damn it!" He stood and ran back into the now much emptier clearing.

Some members of the crowd and the rest of the officers were now beating at the smoking hay. Paxton was securing a pair of cuffs around a still seething Selena and Lance was reciting her rights to her.

I looked back down at Celeste. Her eyes lolled in the back of her head but she was starting to cough.

Sirens screamed in the distance.

The area was awash with light from the floodlights the Conifer PD had erected around the clearing. Trees lining the edge of the clearing on all sides formed a natural perimeter to the crime scene.

Still coughing from the smoke inhalation, I watched the team document the scene, having declined the oxygen the medics had offered. One officer picked up two smoldering books. Another placed a large tome and a small notebook into evidence bags. Behind them, the stake smoked into the night, a solitary sentinel over the proceedings.

I glanced behind me at the ambulance parked a few yards off. Celeste was sitting on the back edge with a shock blanket wrapped around her shoulders. Her hair was hanging in loose curls around her shoulders. A few streaks of grime marked her face, but otherwise, she looked lovely despite the ordeal she had just undergone. She was talking to Lance who was standing beside her. Aside from stepping away for a moment to give out orders to his team, he hadn't left Celeste's side. Lance leaned down and the two of them shared a deep kiss.

Sucking on my lower lip to hide a smirk, I looked around as a loud bang on the side of a parked van echoed across the field. An angry scream followed the banging.

"Ugh, let me go!" Selena writhed against the grip of the officers on her arms as they were putting her into the van. "I have friends in high places that will release me from this! Let me out of here, I demand it!"

A tall, uniformed man rolled his eyes at me as he passed. "I'm going to go shut her up. All that ruckus is distracting."

I watched him walk away, his long blond hair swaying as he walked towards the van. His hands were tucked in his belt. The index finger on his left hand was missing. I contemplated following him when someone touched my shoulder, making me jump as I jerked around.

"It's just me," Paxton said.

I released a breath which triggered another coughing fit. Paxton rubbed my back and my coughing subsided. "You alright?"

I nodded. "You?"

He nodded back. "The team just finished the initial sweep of the Shipyard."

"How was it?"

Paxton grimaced. "I think we may have found the remains for all the bodies that were unaccounted for."

My eyes widened. "Are you serious?"

"It'll take a while to document them all, but... yes, I think so."

"Damn," I exhaled. "How did they get them all here undetected?"

"Just like we suspected. That back road that we first came onto when we came to the estate. Remember how upset Selena was that we were at that gate?"

She had seemed angrier than the situation warranted. I thought about the third symbol in the pattern, same as Morgana's ledger. *Betrayal.*

"Were the bodies still intact? Or were they, uh, processed?"

Paxton grimaced again. "I think you'd rather not know."

Another shiver ran over me.

Paxton rubbed a hand across my back again before catching sight of something behind me. "Looks like Celeste is alright."

I turned back towards the couple behind us, still kissing. "I have a feeling that things will be a lot better for them both going forward."

"Get a room!" someone shouted from the field.

Celeste and Lance broke apart, looking around slightly dazed. They saw me grinning at them and Paxton giving them a discreet *nice one* hand gesture. Celeste hid her face by looking down and Lance turned scarlet. He said something to her before walking towards us.

"Not a word," he muttered.

Paxton said, deadpan, "Yet, the word 'finally' comes to mind."

"Shut up," Lance said, failing to hide a bashful smile. "What's the status on the shipyard?"

I wandered towards Celeste as Paxton started describing what they had found. Banging still came from the van, and the whole back was swaying with the force of her anger. Her cursing had now given way to grunts and screaming.

Celeste was still looking down as I approached, her ankles

crossed as she swung them forward and back. As I sat beside her on the edge of the ambulance, she glanced at me.

"You could say 'I told you so' and I would absolutely deserve it," she said.

"I get the feeling that with you, it's rare for someone to have that privilege."

She snorted. "You could say that too."

I laughed. "He seems a good guy. And he's wild about you."

"Yeah." Celeste sighed, looking up and gazing at the back of Lance's head. "I definitely could do worse." Her eyes twinkled when she gave me a sidelong glance. "So you and the FBI agent, huh?"

I glanced at Paxton's profile, admiring his strong chin and the curve of his mouth as he spoke. "Yep."

"I can tell he's wild about you, too."

I looked back at her. "Oh yeah?"

"Sure. He's so protective of you. It's the way he looks at you, that I can tell. I've never seen a guy so nonchalantly mindful and aware of his partner."

Warmth blossomed on my cheeks and in my chest. "Yeah, he's kinda the best."

"I guess the police sort really don't have a type, huh?"

"Their choice of partner is always surprising."

Celeste laughed and a sense of solid camaraderie formed between us. But then her smile vanished and her eyes glistened in the glow from the floodlights.

"I never thought that Selena could... not after growing up together. We were rivals sure, but we were both Morgana's chosen. Which I guess primed her to be my worst enemy." Celeste sniffed, turning her head away as she wiped her cheeks with her fingers. "In all our years of rivalry, I never would even have dreamed of it coming to this." Her breathing became uneven and I ran a hand up and down her shoulder. For several minutes I worked on keeping my own tears from spilling over as she cried into her hands.

Then her breaths evened out and she sat up. She gave me a

watery smile and wiped her nose on her sleeve. "Thanks. I needed that."

"And I'm sure you will again. Don't keep it in— bottling emotions is bad for you."

Celeste chuckled before she gave me another side eye. "You didn't buy what I said about the coven, did you?"

"What coven?"

I met her gaze, a silent understanding forming between us.

Celeste reached over and grabbed my hand. "Thank you. For everything."

"It's what we do."

After a moment Celeste brow furrowed. "What happened to the guy Selena was working with? Did you guys detain him?"

I froze. "What do you mean?"

"The guy who abducted me. He had nine fingers. Where is he?"

My mind started reeling, putting pieces together. And I realized it was too quiet.

The banging and angry screaming had ceased for some time now. In the distance, we could hear a car accelerating. None of the cruisers or cars had left the clearing.

I jumped up and ran to Paxton and Lance. "I want to talk to Selena. Celeste says there was another person involved. It wasn't Selena that brought her here but a man. I think I saw him head towards the van that's holding Selena."

Lance gave a nod and the three of us walked towards the van at the edge of the clearing. Earlier, I had witnessed the van swaying from the force of Selena's anger. It was as still and silent as a tomb now.

We walked up to the back of the van. The only sound was that of our own steps and breathing. Lance stepped forward, hand on his holster, opened both back doors. A faint waft of hazy perfume escaped as he did. He drew a sharp inhale and Paxton stepped in front of me, shielding me from the van's interior.

But not wanting to miss anything, I stood on the tip of my toes and looked over his shoulder.

Selena was slumped against the right-side wall, her hands handcuffed behind her. A line of blood trickled from the bullet hole in her left eye.

34

Brutus

BRUTUS ACHED ALL OVER. HE WASN'T AS YOUNG AS HE ONCE WAS
and sitting a damn desk job didn't help any. He rolled his shoulders
as he watched the monitor to the interrogation room.

What could McCannon hope to gain from the prisoner that Dr.
Grace couldn't?

Still, it was like he said. He had to talk and then everything
would be green. All their problems would be solved.

Brutus continued to watch the monitor. McCannon was sitting,
poker straight in Dr. Grace's usual chair. He had a stack of papers in
front of him and was hitting the table with his pen, the only sign that
he was agitated. The prisoner on the other hand was leaning back on
his side of the table, languid as he pleased. His feet were even
propped on the tabletop, for pete's sake. He was never that rude to
Dr. Grace.

Brutus wondered what it was about the doctor that demanded

respect from the likes of the prisoner. Brutus respected her, incredibly much so. All that work she had put into helping the FBI. All the hours she had dedicated to researching her book, though Brutus wouldn't tell a soul about that, scout's honor. His admiration for the doctor was the only reason he felt the teensiest little bit guilty over what he was going to do.

Brutus's thoughts drifted to his daughter. It was just that morning he had gone to see her. He hated seeing her with all them tubes and monitors attached to her. Her silky hair had turned brittle and thin, falling out in clumps on her pillow. She had been so scared about that, losing her hair. She thought her teeth might go next, sure of it since she'd had so many dreams about it. But Brutus had assured her she wouldn't lose her teeth. It was common to have dreams about that when a person was stressed.

Brutus would assure her she wouldn't lose anything else, not even another day off her life.

No matter the cost, she would live. Even if it meant he would never see her again.

He sent up a prayer that he would have the strength to do what needed to be done.

McCannon stood. The prisoner nodded, waving a lazy hand as the director moved towards the door. The prisoner also got up, turned, and exited the room through the other door into the detention side of the facility.

Brutus pressed a button. From the hallway, he heard the seal around the door hiss. Slow, heavy footsteps echoed down the hall as McCannon walked forward, finally coming flush to the little closet that was Brutus's office.

He spun around in his chair to face the doorway. "Hey, boss." He hoped the director wouldn't notice the sweat starting to break out on his brow.

"Hey, Brutus." Dark circles ringed McCannon's eyes, an accessory to his ever-stoic demeanor.

"Didn't go so well?" Brutus asked.

McCannon smacked the stack of papers in one hand against the palm of his other. "No. He's more receptive to Dr. Grace."

"That's frustrating, sir. Why isn't she here? I haven't seen her in a while."

"She's been requested on another case down in Conifer. Required her and Agent Holt's particular skills. Hopefully they'll wrap that up quickly so we can keep picking at the gold mine that's the Recruiter." McCannon took a step towards the outer door. "How's your kid doing?"

"She has her good days and her bad days. Today's been a bad day." Brutus raised his shoulders, betraying the ache in his heart. "But we'll make it through this, sir. She's as tough as nails and I have a good feeling that she's going to have more good days than bad going forward."

McCannon nodded. "I'm glad to hear that. You take care and you let me know if you need anything. I'll see to it personally that it's taken care of."

A lump formed in Brutus's throat. "Thanks, sir. Have a good day, now." He pressed a button and the outer door hissed open.

McCannon nodded again and headed out.

Damn if he didn't have a good boss. If it had been possible for McCannon to help him, he would have taken him up on that half-empty offer long ago.

But it wasn't possible. So Brutus had to take matters into his own hands.

Tumbleweeds might as well have blown across the monitors. Not a single other soul in the building this late in the evening. Even the front desk crew had closed shop hours ago. Just him, the night guard, and the prisoner.

The parking lot's monitor showed McCannon sliding into his car. He delayed leaving for a few minutes but soon put his car in reverse and left the parking area. After about ten more minutes of waiting, a black Porsche pulled into the lot. Its driver flashed the brights twice before turning off the ignition.

Now was the time to act.

Brutus stood, heart trotting in his chest. He sucked in a breath to steady his shaking hands before he shut off all the cameras in the building and deleted the recorded footage for the past day. Turning from his desk, he made his way back down the hall toward the interrogation room. By now, the guard had returned the prisoner to his cell and was back at his station.

Brutus passed the interrogation room door, stopping in front of the detention area. He punched the code into the keypad mounted on the wall and waited as the door hissed open. Then he entered the guard's breakroom.

Two secondhand couches were arranged parallel to each other, one across the back wall, the other with its back to the entrance. Adrian, the guard on duty, sat on the couch with his back to the door. Brutus moved into the room quietly, passing the mini fridge filled with stale pizza. He eyed the coffee station pot. It was steaming and the fragrance of sour coffee filled his nose as he came closer.

Adrian startled before glancing over his shoulder and grinning.

"Hey, Brutus, what's up, my man? Late night, eh?" His accent clipped the words. He turned back to his magazine. "What brings you in? I just brewed some of that shit coffee if you want—"

His words cut short as Brutus hit him over the head with a baton, a sickening thud cracking against the other man's skull. Adrian's overweight body slumped to the side.

Heart now speeding to a gallop, Brutus walked forward and felt through the folds of Adrian's neck for a pulse. A rhythm vibrated beneath his fingertips. He allowed himself to relax.

Brutus turned to the door on the left wall and walked through it to the short hall and another sealed door that opened into the space between the secure side and the interrogation room.

Approaching the keypad on the left, Brutus hesitated.

There would be no going back after this.

Chest constricting, he pulled his shirt sleeve down over his fingers as he pressed the code in. A hissing sound escaped as the door unsealed, and he pushed it open.

The door gave way to a twenty-by-twenty foot room. Along one side of the ten foot glass barrier was a metal receptacle used to pass food trays through each side. Brutus glanced behind him to the upper right corner where he knew a nonoperative camera was hidden. He then walked towards the glass, spotting a neatly made bed, a sink, and a half wall shielding the toilet in the left corner.

On the right side, on top of a desk was a neat stack of printer paper and a number two pencil. The prisoner sat in front of the desk, facing the glass. He smiled as Brutus approached the see-through barrier.

"Good evening, Brutus," Kincaid said.

Sweat had started dripping down Brutus's forehead as he nodded a greeting. "Evening." He cleared his throat to keep his voice from cracking. "We only have a few minutes. Are you ready?"

"Is my transportation here?"

Brutus nodded. "Just pulled in."

"Then I await you, Brutus."

Gulping and heart now cantering, he stepped towards the metal receptacle and pressed the big button flush with the wall with his sleeved forearm. A humming sounded and the glass wall slid to the right, opening enough for someone to walk through.

Kincaid stood, straightened his prison jumpsuit, and walked to Brutus. "Lead the way."

Back through the doorway, up the hall to the guard's lounge area. Kincaid let out a short exhale through his nose at the sight of Adrian slouched on the couch with his mouth hanging open, but otherwise he made no sound as he followed Brutus through the room and up the secure corridor before stopping at his office. He turned to face Kincaid.

Kincaid inclined his head. "Thank you, Brutus. Your aid has been most helpful."

Brutus pulled out his gun from his holster and handed it to Kincaid. "You won't forget our bargain?"

"There's already a team working on your daughter as we speak."

Brutus's own heart dropped as he sank into his desk chair. "And she'll live?"

"I guarantee it."

Brutus nodded. He looked up to the ceiling, sending up one last prayer for his soul, before he pressed the button. The metal door hissed again and opened.

"Make it quick," Brutus said.

Kincaid nodded. "I wish your family well."

A panicked cackle escaped Brutus's lips as he looked at the picture of his family on his desk. His daughter's snaggle-tooth smile was the last thing he ever saw before Kincaid leveled the gun at his head and fired.

35

A few days later...

Holt

"Thanks for meeting us here," Lance said.

Willow bestowed her warm smile on him. "We were happy to."

Lance, Celeste, Willow, and I were sitting around a table in Olympia Coffee Roasters. It was a bright Saturday morning and the place was bustling. Older couples and young families made up a long line by the counter. The air smelled of baked goods, causing my mouth to salivate as I looked around for our order.

I rested my arm on the top of Willow's chair beside me, touching some of the hair splayed over her shoulders. I wanted to run my fingers through it, but I refrained, contenting myself with rubbing a thumb over her right arm.

"How are you doing?" I asked Celeste.

"I'm well, all things considered," she said, and she looked it. Dark circles were under her eyes, but otherwise she seemed content and relaxed. She brought her mug up to her lips with both hands. "My cough from the smoke is mostly gone, thank the stars."

Willow cleared her throat, a faint hoarseness lingering in her voice. "Better than me, then."

A blue and yellow haired barista came over then holding a large circle plastic tray laden with Willow's and my order.

"Hello, Suza," Willow said at the same time Celeste gave the girl a greeting.

"Hi, everyone," Suza smiled. "I didn't see you guys come in! Ms. Black, it's nice to see you, I wondered when you'd be coming in next. Here are your drinks and pastries." She placed mugs and plates in front of us. When she was finished, she squinted at Willow and said, "Were you the one that ordered the half dozen cupcakes to go?"

"Yep, that was me," Willow smiled as she lifted her mug to her lips.

"I'll be sure not to forget those this time." Suza grinned and turned to leave before Celeste raised her hand.

"Wait, Suza?" she said.

The young woman turned back.

"You're getting ready to start school here soon, aren't you?"

"Yep, I start at Conifer next fall." Suza's bright expression dampened somewhat. "Hopefully, anyways."

"Why do you say that?" Willow asked.

"I've been working to save up for my tuition, but..." Suza blushed. "It's slow going."

"I see," Celeste said, giving Suza a beady stare. "How's your mama doing?"

Suza shrugged. "She has her good days and bad days since dad left."

"I see. Suza, I want you to come to my office in city hall after you get off work on Monday." A grin formed on Celeste's lips. "We have a full-ride scholarship for Conifer that'll be open this next school year. I think you'd be the perfect candidate."

The round plastic tray fell from Suza's hand, clattered to the linoleum and rolled across the floor.

"Oh, sorry!" Suza ran after it and grabbed it before it stopped on a patron's feet. "Excuse me, sorry about that," she said to the older lady before turning back to our table, face now beet-red. "Ms. Black, do you mean it?"

Celeste let out a charming laugh. "When have I ever not meant something I said? I'll see you on Monday."

Suza held the tray to her chest, sobbed out a nearly incoherent thanks and something about calling her mom, and dashed away.

Willow grinned at Celeste. "That was kind of you."

Celeste waved a hand. "I still owed that girl for getting that note I wrote to you guys."

"Kind, beautiful, and generous," Lance said, grabbing her hand. Celeste winked at him.

"How did wrapping up the case go?" I asked before the two of them got lost in first-love dream land.

"We're still working on that," Lance said, tearing his gaze away from Celeste's. "Paperwork, paperwork, paperwork."

I chuckled. "The dream, then."

"We're stuck on a few things still, but we got the autopsy report back on Vyvan along with the documentation of the shipyard." Lance pulled a folder from under his chair and handed it to me. "Anything look familiar?"

I scanned through the documents and nodded. "I knew it."

Willow looked over my shoulder. "Knew what?"

"Same surgical methods used on Vyvan and Morgana as on all the other trafficking victims. Both in the Shipyard and our cases in Seattle."

"But how could you know that?" Celeste asked.

Lance puffed his cheeks before letting an exhale out. "Believe me, you'd rather not know more specifics."

"But wasn't it Selena who had done the, uh, organ retrieval?" Willow asked. "Her perfume was at all the crime scenes. It made sense for it to be there at the last two, but I recognized it from the first scene when we met her. I should have realized sooner. Regardless, how did she know what methods to use?"

"You know we found the ledger at the crime scene. Dr. Abernathy's translation was on Selena's person when we arrested her," Lance said. "There were some pretty graphic descriptions of organ retrieval inside. She probably learned a thing or two from there."

Celeste had turned from the conversation at the mention of Selena and was looking out the window.

Lance tightened his arm around Celeste. "I'm sorry, baby."

"I just..." Celeste shook her head. "It's hard to believe she's gone."

We all sat in silence for a moment.

"But, uh," Celeste took a deep breath. "Selena never had the ledger, remember? Not until after Dr. Abernathy—" Celeste licked her lips, blinking rapidly. "Not until after Dr. Abernathy was murdered. It was a man who took me from my house to the estate. Selena must have been working with someone."

I raised my eyebrows. "That fits. There's no way she could have been at the Ravenwood Estate giving her statement to the police, and in the woods to attack Kay, *and* at the Abernathy manor to kill off Dr. Abernathy."

"Even a witch can't be in three places at once," Celeste said.

"And her partner might have been connected to the organ traffickers which would explain her unexpected death. She was a liability." Willow grabbed my arm. "The Porche! We know that's how they got Celeste there. That must have been how her partner escaped too."

"We'll need to get this to the Vancouver department." I turned from Willow to Lance. "They'll need to know."

"Already sent." Lance had pulled out his phone and was typing away. "And I've just sent this new info to Director McCannon." He glanced at his watch. "I better get going. This conversation might have been the push I needed to tie up those last few loose ends."

I handed him the folder before standing and shaking his hand. "Thanks, Lance."

"Thank you, Holt." Lance gave my hand a hard and hearty shake before he extended it to Willow. "A lot of things would have ended up differently if it weren't for you two."

He gave Celeste a quick kiss before waving again and heading out, the bell over the door jingling as he left.

Celeste caught my covert grin and stuck her tongue out at me. "Yes, he's a good guy and we're very happy. Shut up, okay?"

Willow laughed as I raised my hands in surrender.

The bell over the door jangled again and a woman with white-blonde hair walked in. Willow made a noise of recognition and waved her hand.

"Cynthia!"

The woman looked around and a smiled. "Willow!"

She walked over and laughed when she saw Celeste. "Ah, my lady! You're here too! It's lovely to see you!"

The ladies both greeted the woman before she fixed her heavily done up eyes on me and gave me a beady look. "You must be Paxton Holt, Willow's lover, yes?"

I blinked at the word 'lover' but since neither Willow nor Celeste reacted to it, I ignored it and nodded. "That's me."

"Wonderful to meet you, darling," she said, voice throaty and sincere.

"This is Cynthia Thorne, Malcolm's girlfriend," Willow told me. "How's business been? I've thought of you after everything..." her voice faltered as she glanced at Celeste.

"Earth bless Morgana." Cynthia sniffed. "But things have been booming. Since Morgana passed away, the store's been thriving. Apparently, the whole town is in on some secret that Morgana was the matriarch of a coven or some such rot. Can you imagine? Anyways, it's been wonderful. Actually, Celeste here is considering becoming my partner, aren't you, my lady?"

"I am," Celeste smiled at Cynthia. "A good investment, I think."

"Indeed it would be. Well, I must fly, my darlings. Cheerio and goodbye!" She waved and left to get in line.

Willow and I looked at Celeste, an unspoken question on the air.

"It would be crazy to think that someone as influential as Morgana Ravenwood was the matriarch of a coven of witches, wouldn't it?" She took another sip from her mug. "But I had a quick interview and chat with my friends on the local press and set the story straight as nails."

"We saw that article," I said.

A news story was aired and several articles published over multiple news stations the morning after events that took place at the Ravenwood Estate. They all covered the murders and grave robbing, briefly reporting that Selena had lost her mind from grief, taking her own life before she could be tried and sent to prison. The nonlocal tabloids had called the case *The Conifer Witch Murders* but the reports were mere speculation, making the case out to be more of a ghost story about witches than anything else.

Celeste scratched a fingernail against the table, her voice pinched as she asked, "Any leads on who did it?"

It didn't take a genius to realize she wanted to know who murdered Selena.

"It's still an ongoing investigation," I said under my breath. "But even still, there's nothing to report. It's a safe guess that Selena's partner was also her murderer. And there's no sign of him. He's vanished."

"I'm sorry, Celeste," Willow murmured.

Celeste sniffed and nodded once. She looked out the window, silent. Willow and I gave her a moment of space as we started on pastries and drank our beverages.

Celeste turned back to us, her face set and serious. "If it weren't for you two, I would be dead, and the fate of my people would have been chaos. That is a heavy debt, and one I will not forget."

She pulled out two parchment envelopes from her bag, each

sealed with a black and gold wax lion insignia. She handed one to each of us.

"Don't open it," Celeste said as Willow started sticking a finger under the seal. "Not now. But should you ever need anything, anything at all, open that, and we will come to your aid." She stood. "You have the word of the new matriarch. May the earth and stars bless you."

36

Holt

Willow and I sat in companionable silence for the majority of the forty-minute ride into Conifer, holding hands over the center console. As I rubbed Willow's knuckles, my thoughts drifted from our conversation at the coffee shop to what had happened earlier this week back in Seattle.

McCannon had briefed us on the breakout. From what we could gather, either Kincaid broke out and killed Brutus, or Brutus helped him out and took his own life. Given that his daughter was miraculously recovering from an unexpected heart transplant, we had our suspicions. Regardless, I had seen the crime scene photos. It put a pit in my stomach just thinking about it.

Willow squeezed my hand, bringing me back to myself. "Something's on your mind. Care to share?"

"Just thinking about what happened to Brutus."

Willow's hands started sweating and she shifted in her seat. "Me too. Or, rather, I've been trying to stop thinking about it. Between Celeste's close call and Brutus's crime scene pictures, I don't know when I'll next sleep."

I nodded. "I know what you mean." Willow gently pulled her hand from mine and began rubbing her palm against her knee. "I'm surprised I haven't heard from Kincaid."

I frowned. "Were you expecting to hear from him?"

"No, I mean that..." She hesitated and I glanced over to see her chewing her lower lip. "Kincaid was methodical, meticulous, and arrogant. With what happened with Brutus..." Her voice cracked. "I guess, it just seems unfinished. Why kill him and not the other guard? And what about all those questions he's asked me about my background? Or the weird messages he relayed through Brutus and McCannon? Why go through all that trouble?"

She was right; the whole thing had a dissonance about it. I grabbed her hand again and pulled it to my face.

"I don't know. But if we know Kincaid, we'll know eventually. I don't know why he's made sport of everything, or why your background was important for him to know. But you're not facing this alone. Remember that." I held the back of her hand to my mouth and kissed it.

She watched and smiled. "I know."

Damn, I really loved her. Keeping her hand steady, I brushed my lips across the back of her ring finger, wondering what her response would be when I brought up the subject of marriage again. I knew for sure that I would never want anyone else but her.

"Did you text Del that we were coming, by the way? I forgot."

Willow nodded, opening her phone and scrolling through whatever menu popped up on her screen. "She's already at Sinsae's house."

~

The sun shined down on us in Sinsae's driveway. Del, Sinsae, Solomon, Willow, and I all gathered around my car after Del put her bags inside the trunk.

Del's head barely made it to Solomon's chest as she gave him a hug. "Bye, Solomon."

He squeezed her back. "Goodbye, friend. You take care now, okay?"

"I'll do my best." Del turned to Sinsae. "Thanks for letting me crash at your place."

"Are you kidding, kid?" Sinsae grinned at my niece. "This has been the best week. We'll have to do this again as soon as you're back from your jaunt to the last frontier."

Del grinned back. "Promise."

"When do you land?" Sinsae asked.

"Should land in Fairbanks later this afternoon."

"And you know who's picking you up?" Solomon asked.

"Yeah." Del nodded. "One of the camp directors. My friend Caroline set up a video call for us, so I was able to meet him and see that he was a real person."

Soloman chuckled. "That's good. Be sure to text us as soon as you've landed."

"And if something's fishy," Sinsae said, "you hightail it outta there and head straight back home."

"Whoa," Del raised her hands in front of her. "You're both mother hens. I'll be okay and I'll be safe." She drew both of them into a group hug. "I'll miss you two worrywarts."

"Not as much as we'll miss you," Sinsae said as they all stepped apart.

Willow caught my eye and gave a covert glance at her watch.

"We better get going if we're going to make this flight," I said. I gripped Sinsae's shoulder and shook Solomon's hand. "See you guys soon."

Willow gave them both a hug and the three of us climbed into the vehicle, with Del in the back.

I pulled out of the driveway and started driving out of town to Seattle.

We arrived at the Seattle airport, parked, and followed Del inside. The three of us waited in line to check her bags. A lump the size of a rock had lodged itself in my sternum as I watched my niece chat brightly with the lady behind the check-in kiosk.

She was really leaving. It seemed as if I had only just gotten her back. I cursed my cowardice at never opening up the lines of communication between us over the years, ashamed that a case was what had brought us back together in the end. It wasn't her fault that she was the last remaining reminder of her late aunt.

Del's bags disappeared around the bend on the luggage carousel. She shifted her personal bag onto her shoulder and led the way to security. She stopped by a large pillar to get out of the way of the growing crowd of people heading to their gates.

Once we stood a little ways from the line, I said, "Guess this is it for a while, huh, kid?"

"Guess so." Del watched the crowd, shifting her weight from one foot to the other before turning back to the two of us. "Thanks for the ride."

"Anytime."

Del sniffed and, for the first time in months, her eyes welled with tears. "I'll miss you guys."

Willow stepped forward and folded Del into such a tender embrace that the tears started falling down Del's cheeks and onto Willow's jacket. "We'll miss you, too. *I'll* miss you."

"I know this is a good thing." Del looked up at me, her arms still around Willow. "But damn does this hurt. I wasn't expecting leaving to be so hard."

Willow smiled and tightened her hold on Del. "There's nothing to be ashamed of. This is the physical embodiment of one chapter of your life closing. Of course it's gonna be hard. But you're a tough cookie, and I think this is the best decision you could have made for yourself." She squeezed again and the two broke apart.

Del let out a watery chuckle. "You think?"

"Definitely." I stepped forward and wrapped my arms around her shoulders. "As much as I hate that you're running off to the last frontier, and I won't be an easy call or car ride away, I am so proud of you. I've watched you live through not one, but several of the most challenging things someone can go through and you've come through it stronger than ever. You're one of the most amazing women I know."

Del had tensed under my words, and I could tell by her short, focused breaths that she was trying not to burst into tears. I put my mouth into her hair and whispered, "I will always be here for you. I love you, kid."

A quiet sob escaped Del before she buried her face into my neck, her bag falling off her shoulder and onto the floor. "I love you too, Uncle Ax."

I held my niece for what felt like hours, trying to put everything I had just said into the embrace, wanting her to know that she wasn't alone in this world. She had family who cared for her. Come hell or high water, I would not abandon her again. Willow placed her hand on my back, and I drew strength from her touch.

After a few minutes, Del pulled away and picked up her bag.

She wiped at her red-rimmed eyes and nose. "I gotta find my gate and grab a coffee beforehand, so I better get rolling."

"That mocha coffee place in the main terminal is amazing," Willow said, her cheery tone easing the sad atmosphere.

"The place where you can choose the percentage of chocolate in your drink? I forgot about that." Del grinned at both of us. "Thank you. For everything."

Willow wrapped her hands around my arm. "Let us know when you land."

Del nodded, a small, amused smile growing on her lips. Damn, she looked just like her late aunt when she did that. But this time, the reminder didn't hurt.

"The minute I land, I'll text." She started walking to the line before turning back around and darting back to us, pulling us both into a group hug.

"Last hug," she said, squeezing.

Willow laughed as we squeezed her back.

After we all let go, she turned and walked up to the line. Willow and I moved over to keep her in sight as she weaved through the line barriers.

"She'll be okay," Willow said. "I have been down the road she is on, but I didn't have an amazing uncle to reach out to when I needed it."

I gripped her hand. "I know."

Before Del made it to the guard, she turned, her eyes wide and nose flared. "Willow! When that man asks you to take a leap of faith, you better say yes!" She held up her hand and wiggled her ring finger up and down.

We both let out a huff of air, amused.

"I'm sure I will," Willow said, and gave me a smile.

Del turned and gave her ID to the guard to scan before we lost sight of her.

A swooping sensation flowed through my body. I felt lighter than air, so much so I couldn't even be annoyed at Del's intervening.

Willow would say yes to marrying me.

37

A few weeks later...

Willow

I LOOKED AT MYSELF IN THE STAND-UP MIRROR IN MY BEDROOM, appraising the way my new dress rested on my frame.

My phone buzzed on my nightstand, and I picked it up to see a text from Del in my text thread between her, myself, and Sinsae.

DEL:

UM KNOCK OUT MUCH? You look stunning!

I couldn't help but chuckle. I typed a message back.

You think so? Is it too much?

SINSAE:

TOO MUCH? Woman, he'll be rendered incapable of speech apart from grunting like a caveman.

DEL:

Took the words right out of my mouth.

I laughed aloud at that.

Thanks you guys.

My phone chimed with a private text from Del.

I know Ax is really excited about your date
tonight.

I texted back right away.

Any chance of a hint?

No way in heck.

I hate surprises.

Paxton had sent me a text earlier that day to be ready to go out by seven and to dress formally. After tearing through my closet for something to wear, I found nothing and decided to go out and buy myself a new dress. I tried multiple on. The little black dress. The classic red cocktail. But the one that sparked a light in me was a periwinkle number with ruffled sleeves. Before leaving Conifer all those months ago, I never would have worn a dress like it. But now, I was more at ease with the new life I was living. I wanted a dress to symbolize the shift in every part of my life.

I put my phone down and entered my bathroom to do my hair and makeup. About fifteen minutes later, I exited the bathroom and scrutinized my reflection again.

I couldn't deny the girlish giggles that erupted from me as I appraised myself in the mirror. With my hair up in a ponytail with a ribbon, and a little eyeshadow, mascara, and gloss, I hardly recognized myself. I looked... good. Really good.

A knock echoed through my apartment. I glanced at the oven clock as I made my way to the front door. 6:58.

I looked through the peephole and immediately I felt hot all over.

Opening the door, I smiled.

"Hello, Paxton."

Hand still raised from knocking, he stared at me, eyes wide. "You're breathtaking."

He was wearing a fitted suit and holding a bouquet of tulips and baby's breath. I had never seen Paxton dressed up.

But it certainly was a sight I could get used to.

I pulled him inside to the tiled entryway of my apartment, laughing as I closed the door behind him.

"No one's ever called me that before."

Paxton handed me the flowers and gave me an unabashed look-over. "Spin."

I did, feeling heat rush to my face under the weight of his gaze.

He stopped me by putting one hand on my arm and the other at my waist. "Breathtaking." He put his forehead to mine. "And you smell amazing too."

The desire to start giggling again was almost overwhelming, so I stepped into the kitchen and hastened to put the flowers in a vase.

"Where are you taking me?" I asked as I filled a vase with water. "And why all the secrecy?"

Paxton fiddled with the leaves of a plant hanging from the ceiling over my island. "You'll see. Is this—"

"The plant you got me from Huck's Finest? Yes."

"I don't know why I hadn't noticed it there before. Ready?"

"Yes, as soon as I put my shoes on."

Paxton took me to one of the swankiest restaurants I had ever been to. As soon as we entered the building, a valet walked over to us and took our coats, handing us a token to retrieve them later.

Holding his arm out to me, Paxton led the way to the host stand, occupied by a tall man in black suit and bow tie.

"How may I help you, sir?"

"I have a reservation for two at seven-thirty."

"Name?"

"Holt."

"Holt..." The man traced his finger down the page in front of him. "The private balcony, yes. Right this way."

The man led the way through a bright, high-ceilinged room, that glittered from the lights hitting the crystal chandeliers.

"Private balcony?" I whispered as we passed dozens of round tables all occupied by people dressed to the nines.

Paxton grinned and put a hand over mine. "Wait 'til you see the view."

The host escorted us through the dining room, down a short walkway, and out onto a balcony. A single round table covered in a white tablecloth and fine dining ware was set in the center of the open area. Several heat lamps were erected a few feet from the table, basking the area in a pleasant warmth, despite the chilly evening air.

I ran to the edge of the balcony and gasped. The entire city of Seattle was ablaze beneath the setting sun. Streetlamps, headlights, and reflections from the windows acted like stars and reflected off the harbor. The Needle towered in the distance.

"Oh, Paxton." I turned back to see him standing a little ways behind me. "This is incredible."

His expression was filled with tenderness. "I thought so, too."

I gestured to the table and the skyline. "What is this all for?" I asked.

"Happy one year anniversary."

I blinked at him. "What?"

Paxton chuckled at the look on my face. "Today marks one year since you and I got together."

"From what I recall, you never actually asked me to be your girlfriend, so what are we basing this off of?"

"Touché. Since our first kiss then."

He grabbed my hand and pulled me into his embrace.

I wrapped my arms around him too and felt a square object in his side pocket. My heart skipped a beat.

Into my ear he said, "You're more than what I deserve, better than what I could have hoped for, and beyond what I ever could have wanted. I love you, Willow."

Eyes welling with tears, I squeezed him, my next words feeling less than adequate yet all I could muster. "Paxton, I love you, too."

"I know it hasn't been very long, and God knows how much you and I have been through, but..." Paxton let go and stepped back.

He pulled the object out of his pocket, he got down on one knee.

My breath caught in my throat as my heart began to race. He held the object out in front of him and I saw that it was a small velvet-lined box. I put my hand up to my mouth to cover the grin forming on my face.

His words came out between heartbeats. Slow and fast all at once. "Willow Grace, will—"

"Sir?"

The door onto the private balcony opened and a server stepped forward. Seeing what he was interrupting, his entire face turned a dull red.

I bit my lip to keep from laughing, my own indignation paling to the look on Paxton's face. His shoulders lowered as his eyes widened, a clear sign of quiet outrage.

"My sincerest apologies," the server said, "but there's a call for you up front."

"I'll be there in a minute." Paxton's voice was calm but deep, the way he would talk to the people reporting to him in the field.

"Sir, I'm sorry, but they said it was most urgent you come at once and without delay."

Brows now furrowing in confusion, Paxton stood and looked at the server. "Alright, I'm coming." He turned to me. "Hold that thought. I'll be right back."

I smiled as he walked away, adjusting his suit jacket as he followed the server back into the restaurant.

Turning to the skyline, I took a moment to catch my breath. My head spun in a daze and I held my hand to my face to keep from giggling. The subject of marriage had come up again a few times in as many weeks. My opinion of it had shifted since our several close encounters with death. Paxton's opinion of it seemed to have shifted, too. Joy radiated from within me and I spun around in a circle.

Willow Holt. There was a certain ring to it. Would I keep my name or—

The sound of the door opening again reached me.

"That was quick—" I turned to face Paxton. I froze at the sight of someone else.

A tall man stood in the doorway. His brown hair rustled in the wind and the reflection of the lights made his hazel eyes sparkle. A slow, familiar, kind smile spread over his face.

"It's been a long time, Willow."

I stepped backward, wrapping my arms around myself. My back collided with the railing, the only thing keeping me from falling off the balcony and into the darkening city. I looked down behind me, imagining how far that fall would be before turning back to the stranger in front of me. It didn't look like he had a gun, but I couldn't tell for sure. Maybe he had one tucked behind his shirt. I looked over his shoulder into the dimly lit restaurant.

Where is Paxton?

"I'm sorry to startle you like this," the man said, "I just—"

"How do you know my name?" I asked.

"You won't remember, but we've met. My name is Walter Peirce." He released a breath and ran a hand through his hair. "I'm your father."

A car horn blared from the city below. My breath caught in my chest and I forgot how to breathe at all. My mind went completely still. I had no idea how to register the words he just said, nor what he'd meant by them.

What a famous line that was. In how many movies or books had it been used? And how many children had denied it, screaming, crying, begging. Yet I remained still, unable to utter any word or noise in response.

"I'm sure you have a million questions," Walter said, "and I will answer every one of them. But we don't have time." He stepped forward, I wrapped my arms around myself tighter. "You have intimate knowledge of Terrance Kincaid, the Recruiter. You know he has a web bigger than we can comprehend. One of his next targets will be Winnie Peirce. I need your help to find her before he does."

He ran a hand through his hair again, this time with his left hand. His ring finger was missing, just below the last knuckle.

I sense you'll find her, Morgana had said. *But not in the way you would ever expect. Look out for the nine-fingered man.*

Pushing against the walls of my mind, I forced it to start working again. "I-I don't know you," I said, clenching my clammy hands into fists. "How do I know I can trust you?"

"You don't." The man walked over to the balcony beside me, placing his hands on the banister. His missing finger drew my eyes again. His hazel eyes, fixed on me, drew me back. "You have nothing to fear from me. But the longer we wait around, the bigger the target on our back gets. I'm sorry to have tied you up in this already. But will you take a leap of faith, and come?"

It couldn't be. Not *this.*

I looked at the table behind this man claiming to be my father, to the door, and then back to him. "What about Paxton?"

"It was my men who made the call he's answering. Better he doesn't get involved for his own protection. My people and the FBI... don't get along." The man turned to me. "I know this is a lot to take in, and a hell of a lot more to ask, but I need you to decide. Are you coming, or no?"

My mind reeled. This couldn't be happening. I scrunched my eyes closed, forcing myself to analyze this situation from all angles. If this man was lying, he'd had ample opportunity to hurt me already.

But why would he lie? To claim to be someone's parent was a ludicrous thing to claim... unless...

Unless it was true. Or he was hiding something even bigger than I could imagine.

"Is Paxton safe?"

The man nodded, placing a hand over his heart. "I know it means nothing to you now, but you have my word that he is and will be safe."

Tears formed in my eyes again as I looked around the balcony, thinking how mere minutes ago my life was heading in entirely the opposite direction. Paxton would have proposed, uninterrupted, and I would have accepted without hesitation. He'd stand and swirl me around, laughing, before kissing me and slipping a ring on my finger. Happiness was so close I could still taste it.

How, now, I would be causing the love of my life more pain than I thought possible. Leaving him with his beloved gone and no answers for the second time in his life.

But I had to find Winnie.

I turned back to the man, letting the tears fall.

"I'll go with you."

Did you enjoy *Rite of Grace?* Leave a review and tell us what you think!
https://a.co/d/bZoF6mG

ACKNOWLEDGMENTS

Fiona, you've the patience of a saint. Maybe one day you won't have to yell at me in the comments because I will have finally gotten your astute editorial feedback through my thick skull.

Brian, you've helped me from struggling to walk to running as a writer. As I start to sprint, I'll be thinking of you.

Barbara & Blaze, my beloved proofers! Your feedback is equally hilarious and so, so encouraging. Thanks for being the first of my readers.

Seth, how valuable your time, feedback, and ground support is to me! Thank you, thank you, thank you! (P.S. To Murphy and Sainz: it was his idea. That's all I'll say.)

My team at LMP– I'm here because of you. You rock (but you already know that).

Cole – darling, your encouragement and constant supply of sweet little caffeinated treats was the foundation for this book. I love you, dearly.

Lastly, to the One above. Hallowed be Your name.

Willow Grace FBI Thrillers

Shadow of Grace

Condition of Grace

Hunt for Grace

Time for Grace

Piece of Grace

Flight of Grace

Rite of Grace

Heatwave

Burnout

Deep Heat

Fever Pitch

Storm Surge

Night Watch

Gilt Edge

A Willow Grace FBI Thriller by C.C. West

Shadow of Grace

Condition of Grace

Hunt for Grace

Time for Grace

Piece of Grace

Flight of Grace

Rite of Grace

Lost Grace

Ava Cortes CBI Thrillers

Deep Dark Lies

Dark as Pitch

Join Without Warrant's private reader group on Facebook!

ABOUT THE AUTHOR

 Christyn writes mystery thrillers, which, given where you're reading this, is a logical conclusion to come to. Her introduction to the author world was through the Willow Grace FBI Thrillers, of which she has written three books. She also dabbles in fantasy and historical fiction. Having grown up overseas, graduated from the University of Arizona, and now being a resident of Alaska, she has many interests including but not limited to: Shakespeare, calligraphy, and blueberry picking.

 instagram.com/c.c.westauthor

 facebook.com/author-cc-west

JOIN WITHOUT WARRANT'S MAILING LIST

Follow the link to stay up to date with Without Warrant!

https://BookHip.com/WKDXPAV

You'll receive a **free** copy of

Hard Line: A Kenzie Gilmore Prequel.